No Ties

Spirit Creek Series, Book Four

BRENDA SINCLAIR

To Nita
Happy Reading!
Brenda Sinclair

ISBN 978-1-926474-00-7

DEDICATION

To all breast cancer survivors
and those currently fighting this horrific disease.

Special mention to some survivors and good friends:
lifelong BFFS Lori Fehr Christensen and Sharon Vierboom;
breast cancer advocate, blogger and public speaker Jenn McCrea;
fellow authors and CaRWA members Roxy Boroughs
and Victoria Chatham.

Never give up the fight! We need a cure!

ACKNOWLEDGMENTS

Thank you to Victoria Chatham, Sharon Vierboom and Cathy Keevill for beta reading. I appreciate you spending a little time with my characters and providing constructive critiques.

Thank you to Ted Williams for his excellent line editing. And thank you to the talented Su Kopil from Earthly Charms at http://www.earthlycharms.com for the exquisite cover.

Thanks also to the friendly folks in Miles City, Montana including the hotel proprietors, the waitresses at the various eating places, grocery store clerks, and everyone who provided directions and answered my inquiries during my two visits to your fine town. I enjoyed myself immensely while completing my research, once in early May and again a few years later during a chilly October.

During both visits to Miles City, I checked out the Range Rider Museum over on West Main Street. What a lovely facility! The knowledgeable folks working there patiently answered my questions and often volunteered additional information and insights into the topic at hand. Thank you so much! Readers, if you find yourselves in Miles City and you're of a mind to shake hands with history, wander on over and spend a few hours walking through the various interesting displays. You won't be disappointed.

Thank goodness, I also dropped by the Miles City Library and talked with the very helpful and well-informed librarians. The Montana room upstairs is a goldmine for someone like myself doing research on the area history. And the rolls of microfilm, especially the old newspapers from my era of interest, were invaluable. I'm certain your town is understandably proud of that library.

NO TIES

CHAPTER 1

Spirit Creek, Montana
Saturday, March 19, 1892

Ivy Patterson strolled down the wooden boardwalk, having chosen to take the long way from the schoolhouse to the town's business section. Gazing across the wide street, Ivy noticed a fellow riding by on a spirited, pinto-colored horse. The slightly dusty trail coat and well-worn Stetson suggested he was just a drifter.

She took another look. The fellow sat tall and straight in the saddle, his chiseled jaw and wavy light-brown hair peeking out from under his hat. Ivy halted in her tracks. Could it be him? She hadn't seen him in ten years. With his hat pulled down to shade the morning sun, she couldn't be certain unless she saw his entire face.

She checked the bejeweled watch pinned to the bodice of her dress. Eleven forty. The general store closed for the noon hour. Ivy quickened her pace, navy-blue calico skirts swishing in her haste. A few patches of snow clung stubbornly to the northernmost corners of several buildings. She lifted her skirts and side-stepped a pile of horse manure as she carefully crossed the rutted, muddy street.

It couldn't be him.

But what if it was?

Ivy turned on her heel and retraced her steps, maintaining a suitable distance to prevent him from noticing her in case the fellow proved to be a total stranger. The rider dismounted and tied the horse's reins to the whitewashed hitching post outside The Spirit Creek Hotel. He yanked off his dark-leather gloves and stuffed them into the pockets on his trail coat which he removed and tossed over the ornately-tooled saddle. If it was him, he appeared taller than when she last saw him, slim and fit, with a broad back and narrow hips. He'd matured nicely.

Ivy slowed her pace and paused, pretending to glance into a store window while she observed him through her peripheral vision.

The man ran his hand down the gelding's neck and he appeared to be talking to the animal, although Ivy couldn't hear what he said. She must be mistaken; it couldn't be him after all. Considering the probable example his father would have provided him in his youth, the man she'd believed him to be would never have spoken kindly to any animal. Not like this fellow had.

And then he glanced her way. His facial features were hidden behind a well-trimmed beard and moustache. She hadn't remembered that about him, but he'd been only seventeen years old when she left. She still couldn't be certain if it was him. He didn't acknowledge her, just turned and gazed toward the other end of the street. Seemingly satisfied with what he'd observed, the fellow took the wide wooden steps two at a time and disappeared inside the hotel.

For several seconds, Ivy contemplated what she should do. The slight breeze ruffled her skirts and the scent of fresh-baked bread drifted through the air from the hotel's kitchen, teasing her nostrils and causing her mouth to water. She swallowed hard. Could the fellow be Blake? If so, what was he doing in Spirit Creek? Had he been actively searching for her? Had he somehow discovered her whereabouts? Or had he chosen this town merely by accident?

Ivy's heart raced and her palms sweated. She'd tried so hard to put her previous life behind her, meticulously planned and executed her escape. She hated telling lies, but she'd needed to guard her secrets as fiercely as a mother bear would protect her cub. Just a boring schoolmarm, new to town. Hair in a bun, calico on her back, and wire-rimmed reading glasses had enabled her to fit into her new community without standing out. When asked where she'd come from, a simple 'out West' had sufficed.

No one must ever learn the truth, especially the town's sheriff, Ernest Jones. Although Ernest had been courting her for several months, he still believed Ivy had no ties to family. He certainly didn't suspect her shameful past. And she hadn't confessed otherwise. Due to his occupation, it was imperative that the lawman she loved so dearly never learned the truth!

The stranger's arrival changed everything. Had part of her past just ridden into town? She needed to know for sure, and she wanted to know why. Before she could rethink her decision, she raced up the hotel's steps and snuck inside.

Ivy paused to allow her eyes to adjust to the slightly darker interior. She peeked through the open doorway but the man wasn't registering for a room. No one even stood behind the registration desk. She tip-toed farther down the empty hallway and quickly poked her head inside the dining room. Unobserved, she counted a dozen diners before she discovered the man sitting in the far corner, his back to the wall, gazing into the waitress's eyes.

"What's on the dinner menu, darling?" he queried in a loud, confident voice.

Gertie, one of the hotel's employees, rattled off the trio of daily specials. "Which one would you like, Mr. Robbins?" A beaming smile accompanied her inquiry.

Mr. Robbins? Ivy didn't hear the man's response, her mind racing with questions. She'd been certain of his identity, but now she second-guessed herself. She returned her attention to the interaction taking place between the waitress and her customer. Gertie's mumbled response to something he'd said generated a robust laugh and he slapped one knee.

Ivy gasped and jerked her head back. She would recognize that laugh anywhere. Regardless of what name he used that fellow was Blake Connors. In the flesh. Here in Spirit Creek. But why would Blake provide a false surname? Mind you, she could be accused of the same.

"*What* are you doing?"

Ivy jumped a foot and swung around, meeting eyes with June Davidson, the widowed hotel owner. "My word, you nearly frightened the daylights out of me," blurted Ivy, and then she felt her face redden from her rude outburst as well as having been caught.

"Why are you spying on my dinner customers?" accused June, standing hands on hips. A strand of graying hair escaped the bun at the nape of her neck and she swiped the stray locks out of her eyes.

"I noticed that fellow in the far corner, thought I recognized him.

But I believe I was mistaken," offered Ivy, attempting to justify her little reconnaissance mission. At least, the first part of her explanation was the truth.

Mrs. Davidson stood in the doorway, glancing at the town's newest arrival. "Handsome devil," she observed. "You've caught Ernest's eye, but if things go south with the sheriff, this fellow might be a candidate for a future courtship."

Ivy gasped. "I couldn't! Ever!" She turned, raced down the hallway, and burst through the double doors to the safety of the street.

* * *

Blake enjoyed flirting with the pretty waitress who'd taken his order for one of the daily specials. He sipped the cup of coffee she'd brought. The girl appeared quite taken with him, almost melting into a puddle of female appreciation at his feet. He considered himself an acceptable male specimen. And he'd enjoyed a lady's company behind closed doors more evenings than would be gentlemanly to admit.

He gazed around the dining room, observed the hotel's other dinner guests. Old habits die hard. Blake loved his work, thrived on it. But the secret nature of his employment caused him no end of stress. Constantly on alert. Always mindful of something that didn't fit, didn't look right, or didn't feel as it should. To do less could cost him his life. Continually wondering if he'd be recognized.

He took another swig of the best coffee he'd drunk in ages. The waitress approached his table, carrying a plate heaped with food. Two huge, mouth-watering biscuits rode atop a steaming, hearty stew packed with chunks of root vegetables and beef.

"Here's your dinner, Mr. Robbins. I hope you enjoy your meal." She smiled at him, coquettishly.

"Thank you, ma'am. I couldn't be happier unless you were on the menu, too."

Gertie waved off his remark. "Mr. Robbins. What a naughty thing to say!"

"Just teasing, darling." Blake picked up his fork. "No offense intended."

"None taken," assured Gertie. "I've worked here for years, and I've heard it all."

The waitress bustled off toward the kitchen and Blake tucked into his meal. Soon, his mind wandered back to the gal who'd flirted with him. Tall for a girl, pleasant-looking, slim but with curves in all the right places. Blake's man parts had noticed her, too, and he shifted in his chair. If he ever retired from his line of work and decided to settle down, he could see himself married to someone like her. Hard-working, sensible, with a hint of a mischief streak as well.

Blake shook himself from his musings, knowing them to be nothing more than a dream for now. With plenty of work to complete, retirement seemed eons away. He gazed around the room at the collection of folks partaking of their noon meal. He didn't recognize any of them, and that was a good thing.

In truth, he'd been observing the town from several strategic hiding places for more than a week now, watching and recording the comings and goings of citizens and strangers alike. Still, there'd been no sign of the folks he needed to spy on most. Confident the gang of bank robbers was nowhere near Spirit Creek, Blake decided the time had come to put in an appearance in town to foster some acquaintances. Learn a few secrets. Perhaps share a secret or two of his own.

Secrets. His entire life revolved around lies, deceptions, and falsehoods. Of course, his employer rewarded him with a handsome paycheck for it, and for years, he hadn't seen himself doing anything else. But lately, the shine on his line of work had started to tarnish. He needed a change.

"Is there anything else I can get you, Mr. Robbins?" inquired the charming waitress.

"Not a thing, miss. What do I owe for the meal?" Blake grabbed his Stetson off the chair beside him and stood.

The waitress handed him a slip of paper with the total owing hand-printed in neat script. "Thank you, miss. Can't tell you the last time I so thoroughly enjoyed a meal. And I'm not talking entirely about the food."

Gertie shook her head. "Mr. Robbins, you're a terrible flirt, but you're very good for my self-opinion."

"You're a very engaging young lady." Blake touched his hat brim. "You take care now, and I might be seeing you again. A man needs to eat."

"I would like that very much." Gertie smiled and cleared the dirty dishes while Blake wandered out to the registration desk in the hallway.

"How-do, sir. I'm June Davidson and I own the hotel. How was your dinner?" The gray-haired lady accepted the payment for his meal.

"That hit the spot quite nicely. Thank you, ma'am." After complimenting the meal, he headed outside before she could ask a bunch of questions that he'd just as soon not provide answers for.

First order of business was locating the telegraph office and sending an important message that no one could decipher except for the intended recipients. A well-dressed gentleman was heading up the hotel steps as Blake exited the building.

"Pardon me, sir." Blake met the man's eyes when he halted. "Could you direct me to the telegraph office?

The man stuck out his hand. "Robert Rutherford, Spirit Creek's lawyer. You must be new in town."

"Just passing through. Blake Robbins." He shook the man's hand.

A minute later, after receiving directions, Blake collected his horse and rode off in the direction of the telegraph office.

* * *

Ivy struggled to her feet, having employed one of the town's sturdy new benches in the Grayson Gardens Park to pull herself together. Soothed by the birdsong that drifted to her ears from overhead in the tall pines, she took a deep breath. Her heartbeat had returned to normal.

Moments later, she inhaled the brisk spring air as she strode down the wooden boardwalk, distracted by thoughts of the town's handsome young sheriff who'd been courting her relentlessly of late. He'd blushed clear to his hairline the first time he'd asked her to accompany him on a walk. They'd traversed this very park, still under construction at the time. She could count on one hand the number of times Ernest, always a gentleman, had kissed her cheek following an outing together. Ernest Jones loved her as much as she loved him, however, although he'd seldom voiced his feelings aloud.

After classes were dismissed yesterday, Ivy wasn't surprised when Ernest popped into the schoolhouse and invited her to a Jones family picnic to be held in the newly-opened park after Reverend Gerald's Sunday morning church service. Of course, she accepted. Coming from a family of fourteen, Ernest often included Ivy in Sunday afternoon outings with his boisterous clan. And during the week Ernest somewhat scandalously would hold her hand while they partook of an evening's stroll through the town park. The gossips wouldn't dare start rumors, accusing the sheriff of unseemly behavior when in the company of a young lady. Every Spirit Creek citizen knew Mrs. Jones only raised decent, industrious children. Ivy enjoyed Ernest's companionship immensely, often silently questioning how she'd managed to catch the eye of such a wonderful fellow. She couldn't be happier, and she would marry Ernest should he propose some day.

Intent on completing her trip to the general store, she checked the time and headed back toward Main Street to finish her errand. The general store would be closed tomorrow, it being the Sabbath, and she needed to purchase the items on her list and then hurry home to bake a pie for her contribution to the luncheon.

As she walked, she contemplated Blake's sudden appearance in town and what it might mean. If Blake showed his face here, could the others be far behind? She neither needed nor wanted Charlie, Albert or Blake Connors back in her life!

Ivy spotted Blake riding his horse a ways up ahead as she reached for the store's door latch. He halted outside the telegraph office, dismounted, and tied the horse's reins to the hitching post. In an instant, he disappeared inside the small brick building. She nibbled on her lower lip. Was Blake expecting news or sending a telegraph to someone? Curiosity got the best of her.

She raced down the sidewalk. The last snowy remnants of winter crunched beneath her buttoned boots when she scurried into the garbage-littered alleyway alongside the telegraph building. The first spring rains hadn't removed the stench of filth from the air, but she resisted the urge to cover her nose and mouth with her scented handkerchief. Standing on tip-toes beneath the partially-open window, she pinched her nostrils closed with her fingers and craned her neck to listen.

"That's it, sonny?" A wet cough accompanied the old telegraph operator's question.

"Please read it back to me to ensure accuracy."

"Says here *Arrived stop. Suitable stop. Good as planned stop.* Ya signed it *Blake*," recited the operator.

"Perfect. Please send the telegraph at the earliest opportunity. It's imperative that this message gets through immediately," insisted Blake.

Ivy heard coins being exchanged.

"Should I be on the lookout for a reply, sir?"

"No. There won't be any response. Thank you kindly."

Moments later, Ivy heard a door close. She plastered herself against the wall to avoid being seen while contemplating what the message meant and who would receive it. Obviously, Blake *arrived*, but to what purpose she couldn't imagine. And what seemed *suitable*? What had been *planned*? Had another person organized something and Blake believed it to be good? And why had Blake considered the matter urgent? Her mind raced with possible answers and options.

Was the Town of Spirit Creek suitable?

Knowing Blake, she worried that he and the others formulated a plan to rob the Spirit Creek Commerce and Trust Bank. Or could it be something else? Something legal? Ivy knew that possibility was as likely as a second moon appearing in the night sky. Her stomach roiled. She needed to do something, but exactly what that might be she hadn't a clue. She'd complete her purchases at the general store and think on it while at home baking her pie and then pressing her dress.

Ivy raced out of the alleyway and crashed into an extremely muscular chest, nearly knocking the stuffing out of herself. She gazed upward and met Sheriff Ernest Jones' beautiful brown eyes.

CHAPTER 2

"Whoa. Ivy, where are you going in such a hurry?" Ernest steadied her, holding her perhaps a few seconds longer than necessary before removing his hands from around her tiny waist. She'd nearly mowed him down in her haste, but he'd welcomed the excuse to reach out and touch her, a gentlemanly gesture expected of any lawman. At least, that's what he told himself as justification for the thrill that raced throughout his body when her warm body came in contact with his fingers.

Ivy's face reddened. "I'm so sorry, Ernest. I wasn't watching where I was going. Please accept my apology."

"Of course you're forgiven, Ivy." Ernest smiled at the petite blonde-haired, hazel-eyed beauty he'd been courting.

She'd arrived in Spirit Creek a little over a year and a half ago after accepting employment as the town's schoolteacher, replacing Ellie Thomas who'd married the local lawyer. He'd admired her from afar for months, unable to rustle up the nerve to even talk to her. Ivy became a welcome addition to the community: an excellent schoolteacher and a tireless volunteer whenever anyone needed help with a church project or community endeavor.

"Where are you going?" he asked again, recalling the fright she'd given him when she fell ill with that nasty bout of influenza last year, almost dying from an extremely high fever and delirium.

"Just heading to the general store for a few supplies." Ivy blushed prettily. "With my mind preoccupied with other matters, I failed to notice anyone ahead of me."

"I'd prefer being run down by a pretty girl than a runaway team any day." Ernest had cursed himself for his cowardliness for not having so much as spoken to the attractive girl when he'd feared he'd missed his opportunity. What would he have done if she'd passed from this world, lost to him forever? But his prayers had been answered and she'd survived. He'd taken her for a walk in the park a week later, and since that day, he'd courted her every Sunday after services.

Ivy wrung her hands. "I'll watch for passersby and avoid any further collisions with innocent citizens."

Ernest met her eyes. "Is something wrong? You seemed a little frazzled."

"No!" she blurted and blushed.

"Ivy, what's got you in such a state?" Ernest reached for her hands. "You're shaking, sweetheart. Something isn't right."

"I took a short cut through the alleyway. Something frightened me, but it just turned out to be an old stray yellow cat. I may have scared him equally so." Ivy smiled weakly. "Please, don't give it another thought. I'll be fine."

Ernest released her hands, not believing the fabricated story about the cat. Whatever had her upset, she clearly wasn't going to share it with him. "I'd best get back to work then. I'll see you tomorrow for our walk." He touched his Stetson's brim.

Ivy continued on her way without a word or a backward glance.

Ernest admired her from behind as she quickly moved down the boardwalk, skirts swaying with the movement of her hips, heading in the direction of the general store. Something more than fleeting embarrassment over their collision or a cat crossing her path troubled her. He frowned, recalling when he'd mentioned their Sunday walk in the park and she hadn't made any acknowledgment. Did his weekly courtship mean more to him than to Ivy? Was she waiting for him to further their relationship, seal their commitment to each other by a proposal? The thought of marrying Ivy warmed his heart, but contemplating actually proposing to her frightened him near to death. The possibility of her saying no nearly brought him to his knees. His life wouldn't be worth a plug nickel if she turned him down. Was his procrastination the reason she seemed upset? Was she planning to end their courtship?

With unmarried fellows moving into Spirit Creek every other week, sooner or later, one of them would steal Ivy away from him. Not an hour ago, Donald, his brother and the town's deputy, had reported seeing a new man in the hotel, partaking of the noon meal, flirting shamelessly with Gertie. Someone like this stranger could easily catch Ivy's eye.

Of course, if he discovered something seriously wrong had happened in her life, as her betrothed he'd be in a much better position to help Ivy. Ernest renewed his conviction to ask for her hand before it became too late.

* * *

Ivy mentally kicked herself with each step as she strode toward the general store. *Where are you going in such a hurry?* Her heart had almost stopped when she collided with the handsome sheriff, lost in her thoughts.

"Ernest must *never* learn the truth," she whispered the vow aloud. Most certainly, he would refuse to spend the rest of his life married to a woman with her past. Ivy shivered, thinking such dark thoughts. She slipped into the general store, her arrival announced by the tinkle of the tiny silver bell above the door.

"Good afternoon, Miss Patterson." The proprietor's wife, Elizabeth Waverly, greeted her from behind the large wooden counter.

A young boy stood on tip-toes in front of a row of glass candy jars, contemplating his choice while his mother stood patiently waiting for Ronald Waverly, the store owner, to package up her other purchases. Mrs. Waverly bent over a sheet of paper, no doubt tallying up the total owed to apply to the woman's account.

"Hello, Mrs. Waverly," replied Ivy, glancing about the establishment. Floor-to-ceiling shelving was full to overflowing with stocked goods. Everything from flour to canned beans, bolts of fabric to work boots. And items like saddles, tack, barbed wire and tools were stored in a shed behind this building. A customer would be hard pressed to ask for something that couldn't be found for sale here.

Several well-worn but sturdy wooden chairs circled a pot-bellied stove in the middle of the floor where a couple of old-timers sat smoking pipes while heat from the blazing fire warmed their aging bones. She shivered when the scent of their pipe smoke reminded her of early childhood evenings spent at home with her father. Eavesdropping, Ivy discovered today's topic for discussion centered on the plans for a new schoolhouse. The community bigwigs had been arguing over the matter for months, and Ivy figured she'd probably be married before the new building came to realization. She wasn't holding her breath about it.

A minute later with the candy selection completed, the woman and child exited the store.

"How can I help you, Miss Patterson?" inquired Ronald.

"I'm here to pick up a few things: coffee, lard, three pounds of flour, four cans of beans, two cans of peaches, and thick black thread for mending," she rhymed off the items on her list.

"Give me a few minutes, and I'll have it collected up for you." Ronald turned to his wife. "Start the cyphering, my dear."

"Thank you. No need to hurry." Ivy dug in her reticule for her change purse. She didn't believe in buying on credit, a lesson learned from Aunt Minnie Patterson back in California.

Just then, the bell above the door announced another arrival, and Ivy swung around expecting to be greeted by a female citizen dropping by to pick up food items of her own. Instead, a set of hazel eyes identical in color to her own met her gaze.

The fellow stopped in his tracks.

Ivy swallowed hard, her fingers worrying her change purse. Would Blake recognize her? Realize who she was? What would she do if he spoke to her? How would she explain knowing him to Mr. and Mrs. Waverly? She held her breath.

"Ma'am," he mumbled, touching his hat brim. He stepped around her and smiled at the shopkeepers. "Would one of you have a moment to help me select a pair of new boots?"

"I surely would," Elizabeth replied, beaming. "Just as soon as we complete this order."

"Much obliged, ma'am."

Ivy inhaled quickly, certain she'd be turning blue any second now. She clasped the small handful of change in her sweaty fist, refusing to glance his way.

"That will be a dollar twenty," said Elizabeth.

Ivy handed over the exact change. "Thank you, Mrs. Waverly."

Ronald handed Ivy the wrapped package. She turned and almost raced out the door. Thankfully, Mrs. Waverly hadn't spoken her name.

Perhaps Ivy could keep her secrets after all. Blake hadn't appeared to recognize her, certainly hadn't indicated anything by a change in expression. She headed for home, praying her true identity would remain undiscovered.

No one must ever learn that Blake Connors was her brother!

* * *

Blake watched the young woman skedaddle out the door as if the devil nipped at her heels. He smiled to himself, knowing the little minx believed he hadn't recognized her. After all these years, he should have given her a piece of his mind.

Some time past midnight two days after their ma passed, Ivy had dressed herself in a pair of faded denims he'd outgrown, one of his new plaid shirts, and his old felt hat and then silently snuck out of the shack their pa had considered a home. While he understood her motives, he still hadn't forgiven his sister for what she'd done. Blake had been madder than a wet hen, especially about losing his favorite hat.

Neither he nor his pa or brother had seen nor heard from her since. On a hunch, he'd spied on their spinster aunt's home years later and discovered she'd been living there. A few discreet inquiries had yielded further information about his industrious sister who'd taken to using their mother's maiden name, Patterson, as her surname. He'd been surprised to learn that their aunt generously had raised Ivy as her own child, and later paid for Ivy's normal school training with revenues from the boarding house business she'd inherited from her deceased parents, his and Ivy's grandparents. A couple of years ago, Blake had been told by Aunt Minnie's neighbor that Ivy had moved to Spirit Creek to teach school.

His sister looked happy. He'd spied her talking with the town's sheriff a few minutes ago. Blake recognized a man smitten by a female when he saw one. The sheriff definitely loved Blake's little sister. Judging by appearances, Ivy should be receiving a proposal from the fellow before long. Blake chuckled to himself. A Connors marrying a sheriff. Wouldn't that tidbit of information curl their pa's hair, if he ever found out?

"Do you require some new socks, sir?" suggested the storekeeper's wife. "To go along with those new boots?"

"A couple new pairs wouldn't hurt," he agreed.

"Several local ladies knit socks in all sizes for us to sell." The woman hustled toward the back of the store, leaving him to his musings.

Blake couldn't blame his sister for deserting her father and brothers. Ivy had been their mother's favorite, and his sister shared her ma's hatred of the law-breaking. It hadn't surprised him that Ivy took matters into her own hands and escaped the inevitable life that had been her destiny. Although his pa must never know, Blake agreed with his sister's convictions, and he'd found his own way to rebel against the lifestyle he hated.

"Here you go, sir. I'm certain these will fit you." The storekeeper's wife finished wrapping his purchases.

Blake handed over payment in full. "Thank you, ma'am. I appreciate your help."

"You're very welcome. Are you staying in town?" she inquired.

"Moving on for now, I'm afraid. But I will certainly consider dropping by this way again." Blake touched his Stetson's brim, knowing the mixed truth to his statement.

"You have yourself a good day, sir. And travel safely." She handed over his parcel and he turned to leave.

"Bye now," he replied, hearing the suspicion that accompanied her sentiment.

He knew the woman's gaze had followed him as he headed out the door. He didn't doubt the matron's ability to sense trouble when she saw it. And she couldn't be more right.

CHAPTER 3

Sunday, March 20, 1892

Ivy sat beside Ernest in one of the Jones family's pews in The Spirit Creek Church. She hoped her nervousness didn't show. Discovering her brother's arrival in town, and then running into Ernest moments after spying on her law-breaking kin, had left her discombobulated.

Had Blake moved on? Left town and wouldn't be returning? Or had he registered at the hotel and intended to remain in Spirit Creek for an extended period of time? Please, Lord, not the latter. Telling lies. Harboring secrets. Avoiding suspicions. Her mind couldn't take much more of this. But her entire future depended on it.

Her thoughts wandered to childhood days as Reverend Gerald's voice droned on. As long as she could remember, her father had boasted about his expertise as a bank robber. Her mother had detested her husband's chosen profession and constantly begged him to find honest work, to walk the straight path. But no, Charlie Connors had built himself a reputation which he felt honor bound to uphold, taking unexplained pride in his life of crime. The entire matter seemed totally twisted to Ivy's way of thinking.

When her mother passed away days after Ivy turned twelve, she'd immediately planned and executed the perfect escape. Ivy knew in which fancy china sugar bowl her mother had hidden a considerable amount of money. Their emergency fund she'd called it. Ivy suspected her mother considered the money a contingency plan in the likelihood her father would eventually be caught during a robbery and imprisoned. Ivy considered her ma's death qualified as a valid reason to access the funds, and she took the money and ran toward a better life for herself. Ivy hadn't seen her father or brothers in ten years, which suited her just fine.

She gazed around the church, smiling at a couple of friends, namely Dottie Hartley, owner of The Spirit Creek Clothing Emporium, and Sadie Maxwell, recent bride of the oldest Maxwell son, Chance. Just then, the church's heavy wooden door opened slowly, a squeaky hinge calling out for a bit of lubrication. Ivy's heart almost stopped. What if it was Blake? Had he found religion like herself? Attended services regularly? What would she do if he slipped into the pew beside Ernest? Ivy peeked over her shoulder. Her gaze followed Ronald Waverly as he crept down the red-carpeted aisle to the front pew and slipped in beside Elizabeth. Ivy exhaled, unaware she'd been holding her breath.

She straightened in her seat and attempted to listen to the reverend's sermon. She heard something about brotherly love which promptly sent her thoughts spinning back in time again. Brotherly love indeed. As a little girl, she'd adored the younger of her two brothers. Although five years older than her, Blake had spent hours playing with his friends and frequently included Ivy in their antics. Albert was four years older than Blake, however, and Ivy couldn't recall one time when he'd spared a moment for either of his younger siblings. Following their pa around like a faithful hound had consumed Albert's every waking moment, often when he should have been in school. Albert hadn't shown any interest or talent for book-learning, unlike Blake and herself who'd excelled in school and read every book they could lay their hands on.

"Just a couple of announcements before…"

The reverend appeared to be winding down.

Ivy sighed and glanced over, meeting Ernest's eyes. He reached for her hand. She sensed his affection for her as the warmth from his hand traveled through her body to her core. She couldn't love him more. He winked at her and her cheeks warmed. Had anyone noticed his brazen behavior?

"Behave yourself. We're in church," she whispered near his ear so only he would hear.

Ernest straightened in his seat, the picture of innocence. And then he winked at her again.

Ivy glanced at her watch, a graduation gift from her spinster aunt. Five minutes to twelve. She silently cursed her impatience and then prayed for forgiveness. Who was she to rush a man of God at work? Suddenly, everyone stood for the final hymn, and Ivy joined in the singing.

* * *

A half hour later, Ivy clasped Ernest's hand and strolled through the lovely Grayson Gardens Park, proud to be seen with him. He still wore his going-to-church suit and he'd never looked more handsome. The rest of the Jones family were already assembled at the park when they arrived. Only Donald was absent, probably working at keeping the peace in the small town. The toddlers hid behind their mothers' skirts while several young boys climbed trees with the agility of monkeys. The older children entertained themselves with a game of tag with their friends.

Ivy set her peach pie down on a table covered with a rainbow-colored cotton tablecloth. The Jones women had brought enough food for an army, but the entire family was present and Ivy knew from experience that the Jones men enjoyed a hearty meal. Ivy smiled as Doc Benjamin and Pearl's little boy, James, toddled across the grass, taking only a couple of steps before falling on the uneven surface. He giggled, clambered to his feet, and headed for the black and white collie dog he spotted coming down the path.

"Doggie!" he exclaimed, as his father raced to catch up to him.

Mrs. Jones reached for Ivy's hand and squeezed it affectionately. "Thank you for bringing a pie, dear. I know how much you love to bake, and I'm certain it will be delicious, as usual. Now why don't you and Ernest go for a little walk while we set out the rest of the food? Pearl and Agnes and Angela can help me," offered Mrs. Jones.

Ernest kissed his mother's cheek. "That's a wonderful idea. Come on, Ivy, before Mother changes her mind and puts you to work."

Florence Jones snorted. "Off you go, the both of you. But be back here in twenty minutes."

Ernest reached for Ivy's hand and guided her along the stone pathway. "I've been wanting to talk to you alone since you walked into church this morning, wearing that lovely blue dress. Is it new?"

"Dottie, owner of the clothing store, started selling previously-owned dresses to those of us who can't afford her custom-made gowns. She keeps half of the proceeds and the other half goes to the church children's fund."

"What a generous endeavor." Ernest appeared impressed.

"Maggie Carlyle claimed her new-mother's figure wouldn't allow her to button up half her dresses any longer, so she donated several to Dottie's new endeavor. This dress is one of them. Isn't it gorgeous?" exclaimed Ivy.

Ernest winked at her. "Not nearly as beautiful as the girl wearing it."

Ivy felt herself blush. "Sadie Maxwell passed along several of her gowns to Dottie also. Some of those dresses are so fancy, I can't imagine where a person would wear them in Spirit Creek."

"Reckon you could wear them to a shindig at the hotel, maybe a wedding," suggested Ernest.

"I suppose I could. Dottie is quite a shrewd businesswoman. Considering her talent with a needle, she could easily have altered those dresses to fit Maggie and Sadie, but if the ladies donate their old gowns, then who do you suppose they'll hire to design and sew new ones for them?"

"Brilliant indeed," agreed Ernest, reaching over and trailing his hand across her cheek.

"Married to their well-to-do ranchers, the ladies certainly can afford a custom-sewn gown."

Ernest led her down a trail alongside the creek that ran through town. "It's so peaceful here. I just love Sunday strolls in this park."

"Speaking of peaceful, did you happen to notice the stranger in town yesterday?" Ivy silently complimented herself on the skillful way she'd broached the subject most on her mind.

"Donald mentioned something about him having dinner at the hotel. Seemed quite taken with Gertie." Ernest met her eyes. "I haven't seen him though, so he must have moved on already.

"I observed him when I encountered him from across the street. He has shifty eyes and an arrogant swagger. I'd bet my new dress he's up to no good. He could be a cattle rustler? A bank robber? You should run him out of town if he hasn't left yet," suggested Ivy.

Ernest guffawed. "My, don't we have an active imagination. How did you discern all of this by walking past him on the street?"

"I consider myself an excellent judge of character," claimed Ivy.

"Well, my dear, I'm aware of everything that happens around here. And I pay particular attention to the comings and goings of anyone new in town. Donald didn't mention having suspicions about the stranger." Ernest raised her hand and touched his lips to her fingers. "I think you're being unduly concerned about this fellow."

Ivy sighed. How could she warn Ernest to be particularly watchful of her brother without coming right out and announcing the bank would probably be robbed one of these days? She couldn't tell him that her father and brothers, without a moment's remorse, broke the law for a living.

"I just want you to be safe. Never let your guard down, Ernest," pleaded Ivy.

Ernest tucked her hand into the crook of his arm. "I've been especially careful since you entered my life. I won't let anyone get the upper hand with me. I promise."

Ivy's eyes welled and she discreetly dried the unshed tears with an embroidered handkerchief. She prayed Ernest wouldn't be harmed, but she knew he loved being a sheriff. Suddenly, she wondered if her father or brothers had ever killed anyone in the course of their thievery. It might be only a matter of time. Eventually their luck would run out, and someone intent on stopping their crimes would be murdered. She swallowed hard. Maybe even Ernest.

No. She wouldn't allow her mind to even consider such a thing.

Of course, even one of her family members if found responsible for another's death would be punished in due course, perhaps justifiably paying with his own life.

Why had she been born into such a despicable family? And what were they up to now?

* * *

Ernest leaned against a particularly tall evergreen tree, holding his cup of lemonade in one hand and waving to Luke Carlyle's son sitting on a branch of a young maple tree a few feet away. "Careful you don't fall out of there, Sam," he warned.

"I won't." The child waved back.

"Did you climb trees when you were a boy?" Ivy's head tilted to the side.

Ernest straightened and smiled. "You bet I did. Broke my arm once, too. Received a sound tongue-lashing from Mother over that. Cost her one of her prize laying hens to have the doctor come and set the break. Not certain she's forgiven me yet."

Ivy laughed. "Your mother would frighten the spots off a leopard if she were riled enough. Remind me to stay on her good side."

"Mother adores you. I doubt you have any reason for concern."

Ernest slipped his arm around Ivy. He couldn't believe how well she fit in with his family. She accepted their good-natured teasing, giving back a few verbal jabs of her own which only endeared her to them even more. Once he mustered up the courage to propose, she would meld perfectly with the Jones clan from the moment the 'I do's' were spoken.

"Time for dessert. Come on, everyone!" Mrs. Jones waved a tea towel above her head to attract the children's attention.

Ernest and Ivy accepted a piece of her peach pie and then wandered over to a semi-secluded grassy spot where he'd settled a blanket on the ground. Ivy gracefully sat with her skirts tucked beneath her legs. Ernest handed her plate back.

Ivy took a bite. "Oh, my, this is good. I'd hoped I'd used enough sugar."

"Delicious." Ernest winked at her. "You're going to make some lucky fellow an excellent wife some day."

"I'd like nothing better," she whispered, gazing into his eyes.

Ernest blinked and returned his attention to his pie. He'd hoped she would interpret his comment correctly, a means to garner some indication of where her head and her heart were concerning him. If he proposed and she turned him down, he'd never survive the humiliation.

I'd like nothing better. Exactly what he'd wanted to hear. Some day she'd be his, and he couldn't wait to make her his wife. He required a ring for his proposal, the largest purchase he'd ever made. Something that would guarantee a yes from the woman he loved. She deserved nothing less.

He'd saved his money since childhood, fetching for June Davidson at the hotel, and doing odd jobs around town for one merchant or another. And now he deposited his sheriff's wages in the bank every month, only paying for rent and food or necessary clothing, allowing himself one pair of new boots every year. A trip to Miles City seemed in order. For several reasons.

"Have you given any thought to what you'll do about that stranger?"

Ernest almost choked on his sip of lemonade. He'd considered the matter settled, not worth another moment's concern. Why had she become so preoccupied with this fellow?

"Sweetheart, I doubt the stranger intends to do anything illegal. The man simply passed through town, far as I know. Don't worry your pretty head about him. If he's up to no good, I'll figure it out soon enough." Ernest polished off his pie and set the plate aside on the grass.

"But I worry about you." Ivy sighed.

Ernest kissed her cheek. He'd been concerned the fellow might catch Ivy's eye as a possible suitor, but she seemed worried that the stranger might cause trouble. "That's very nice of you. But there's no call for you to be interfering in my law-keeping duties or questioning my abilities as Spirit Creek's sheriff."

"But, Ernest, what if…"

He interrupted, "I'm not in the habit of quizzing you on your methods of teaching the town's youngsters to read and cypher. Please extend me the same courtesy and stop worrying about this fellow."

Ivy blushed to her hairline.

"I apologize if that sounded a little harsh." Ernest reached for her hand. "I haven't seen him, nor has Donald. He's probably moved on, miles from here with no intention of returning. Trust me. I have the situation under control."

Ivy smiled weakly. "I pray you're right," she whispered.

Ernest helped her to her feet and they returned their dishes to his mother.

"I'll walk Ivy home now," announced Ernest.

Everyone in his family extended their goodbyes as the couple strolled down the pathway toward the schoolhouse.

CHAPTER 4

Wednesday, March 23, 1892

Dressed in dusty trail clothes, Blake packed up his bedroll and camp gear, slipped his rifle into the leather scabbard on his saddle, and mounted up. Dammit, he hated sleeping out in the elements, nearly freezing off his behind. But he'd spied on the town for as long as necessary, and he'd learned everything he needed to know. The time had come to meet up with his father and brother, but he certainly wasn't looking forward to it.

"Time to move on, Humbug." Blake grimaced at the stupid name the horse's first owner had given him. There'd been no changing it, but not from lack of trying. He could've continued for all eternity, but the horse would answer to nothing else. *Come here, Humbug.* There was no way in hell he'd be calling him. At least, Blake had been able to train him to come to a whistle.

The pinto thoroughbred mix stepped lively as they covered the miles to their destination. Blake rode in silence, admiring the Montana scenery so unlike back home in California. *California.* It seemed a lifetime since he'd lived there. Every time he faked an argument with his father and rode off in an apparent fit of temper, he'd head off on another job. Then a few months later, he'd return all apologetic and contrite. Soon, his pa and brother stopped questioning where he'd been and what he'd been doing. Sadly, he realized that his kin folk just didn't care.

Blake inhaled a deep breath of the clean, crisp spring air. Of all the places he'd traveled and worked, he loved Montana the best. He could see himself settling down here one day. Maybe find work as a sheriff in some nice little town, marry up with a lovely young lady, and raise a passel of kids. Before he could stop it, a picture of Gertie, her belly swollen with his child, popped into his mind. He shook his head to clear the image and rode on.

Yes, he would settle in Montana if given his choice. Even in spite of the accursed winters. He'd never experienced such a bone-chilling cold in his entire life. He noticed that a few brave crocuses had popped their heads out of the ground, the blue flowers a welcome sight after months of nothing but snow cover. He would swear he detected the scent of sage being carried on the gentle breeze, or it might have been just wishful thinking. In time, new life would return to the countryside, blanketing the rangeland in green vegetation and wildflowers in a riot of rainbow colors.

A half hour later, Blake rode into the Connors camp. A mangy-looking hound with one ear half missing rushed toward him as he dismounted. The animal growled low in his throat and Blake returned the greeting. The critter turned tail and headed back behind what appeared to be a new grub wagon, judging by the collection of cooking pots hanging off one side.

"Where the hell ya bin?" demanded his father, limping toward him and spitting a stream of tobacco juice out one side of his mouth. "Figured ya'd be here a week ago."

Blake stood hands on hips. His pa's clothing hung on a too-skinny frame, and it appeared they hadn't been washed since the day he'd purchased them in some mercantile. Or stolen them off some woman's clothesline. Either scenario seemed a distinct possibility.

"Gosh, it's great to see you again, too, Pa," replied Blake, smiling broadly, knowing a cheerful expression irked the old man something fierce. He couldn't recall ever seeing his father smile.

"Lose the sass, boy." His pa waved one grubby hand in his direction. "Tie up yer horse and come set a spell. Fill us in on what ya learnt."

Blake took his own sweet time unpacking his gear, removing Humbug's saddle and settling him into the roped-off, makeshift corral with the other horses. He grabbed his rifle, strode toward the fire and accepted a cup of coffee from a fellow he'd never seen before. "Thanks," he muttered as he lowered himself onto a tree stump across from his brother. His sibling's clothing wasn't in much better shape than their father's. The smell of Albert's unwashed body drifted clear over to where Blake now sat. Couldn't his brother at least take a dunk in a creek once in a while?

Albert glowered at him and then pointed at Blake's rifle on the ground alongside its owner's foot. "Planning on using that?"

"Only if some unwelcome varmint wanders into camp and requires shooting," he answered, taking a sip of the sludge he'd been offered. He grimaced and set the tin cup aside.

"Four-legged or two-legged?" sneered Albert from his own stump.

"Whichever," replied Blake, purposely keeping his response short and lacking in commitment. Less chance of giving too much away.

Charlie Connors teetered to one side as he stepped around the pile of firewood. He caught his balance and settled on a wide, perfectly-round stump situated beside Albert. "So spill it, Blake. What ya learnt about this Spirit Creek place?" demanded Connors, Sr., crossing his arms and glaring at his son.

Blake straightened his back. "Nice little town, growing every year. Ranching community mostly. Small timber operation to the west. Has all the business enterprises necessary to sustain the population. I met with some of the locals: hotel owner and a waitress, the couple who own the mercantile, a lawyer fellow. All of them friendly, don't suspect nothing." Blake didn't mention that he'd encountered his little sister who was being courted by the local sheriff. His pa would have had a conniption fit over that bit of news. Nor had he volunteered information on the old telegraph operator he'd dealt with.

"Does the damn town have a bank?" growled Charlie, shifting position on the log.

"Of course, it has a bank." Blake shook his head. Dang it anyway, his pa never remembered half of what he told him anymore. When Blake learned about the scheduled upcoming deposit, he'd arranged the robbery himself in hopes of impressing his old man. And with another purpose that would suit just fine.

Charlie's cigar stuck out between his gapped front teeth while he stirred the campfire's embers to life. Flames flared and he added another log. "That special shipment still arrivin'?"

"Yes, sir, right on schedule."

"Good. Then let's get to plannin' how we's gonna steal it."

The log had caught and the fire crackled merrily. Blake stood. "Can I at least get some food into me first?"

"Suit yourself," chimed in Albert, meeting his father's eyes, his adoration obvious. "Pa's the brains of this outfit anyway. Sure as hell don't need you fer no plannin'."

"All right then." Blake wandered toward the grub wagon, shaking his head. If these fools even suspected the extent of his planning, they'd fall off those damn tree stumps.

Monday, March 28, 1892

Ivy set her teacher's desk to rights, having completed her lesson plans for the following day. Considering all the time and energy she'd been expending on worrying about keeping her secrets, it amazed her that she could even concentrate on her work.

Just as she rose to head into her private quarters in back, a loud knock on the door startled her. Her heart leapt into her throat. What if Blake stood outside? What if he'd figured out it was Ivy he'd seen in the general store?

"Who…is it?" Her voice cracked.

Ivy heard no response and she nearly fainted from nerves.

"Who is it?" she repeated the question more forcibly.

"It's me, Ivy. Please open the door, my hands are full."

Ivy blew out her breath, recognizing Sadie Maxwell's voice. Having turned her life around after facing horrendous personal tragedies, Sadie Peterman had married Chance Maxwell, the oldest Maxwell son, and she now lived on the Circle M Ranch with her husband and stepson. Sadie and Ivy had become good friends while working on several community projects together.

"Coming, Sadie." Ivy hustled over to the door and flung it wide open.

Sadie stood with her arms laden down with what appeared to be ladies' clothing.

"Goodness sakes, Sadie. What on earth have you got there?" Ivy's hand grabbed a lacy white shawl about to land on the dirty classroom floor decorated in small muddy shoeprints. She'd forgotten to mop the entryway after the children left for the day.

"Let me carry these straight through to your room and set them on your bed and then I'll explain." Sadie brushed past her, set on her mission.

Ivy followed like an obedient puppy.

Seconds later, a mound of clothing landed atop Ivy's narrow cot in her living quarters.

"Could you please explain this now?"

"Certainly," began Sadie, breathlessly. "I've brought you some of my less fancy dresses and petticoats and that shawl. It's absolutely ridiculous that you should be paying for used gowns at Dottie's emporium, when I have all these dresses that are ideal for you."

"Now, Sadie, I don't mind paying for…"

"Nonsense! I was employed for a short spell as a substitute teacher and I know what meager wages a schoolteacher earns. If you're going to rope in Ernest Jones, you require the proper clothing." Sadie beamed. "Consider this my little donation to the effort. I want you to be a married lady by year end."

Ivy giggled. "I wasn't aware someone initiated a contest complete with a deadline."

"Nothing official. No bets being placed. At least, not that I know of." Sadie winked at her. "You and Ernest are perfect for each other. I just want the two of you to be as happy as Chance and me."

"From your lips to God's ears," mumbled Ivy. She'd like nothing better than to become Mrs. Ernest Jones.

Sadie slumped into one of the pair of rickety wooden chairs at the kitchen table. "Goodness, being a mother-to-be is exhausting work." She dug a lacy handkerchief out of her reticule and dabbed at her damp forehead.

"Forgive me for not even offering you a cool drink or a chair." Ivy scrambled to fetch her friend a glass of water.

Sadie waved off her concerns. "Don't worry. I feel as big as a house, but Doc assures me I've still two months to go. I'm concerned there are twins in here." She patted her already ample middle.

"Oh, Sadie!" exclaimed Ivy. "Wouldn't that be wonderful?"

Her friend scowled. "Only if you come out to the ranch and help with the two a.m. feedings and wash all those diapers."

Ivy handed her friend the water glass. "You have a point there.

Perhaps one son at a time for Chance will suffice."

"My thoughts exactly," agreed Sadie, downing the water and setting the glass on the table. "Now, let me see you in the pale green dress first. That's always been one of my favorites."

"You don't mind parting with all of these?" Ivy dug though the pile of clothing, recognizing several items she'd seen Sadie wearing on one occasion or another before her middle had expanded with child.

"Oh, pooh. I've more gowns than I could ever wear in three lifetimes. Why father indulged me in such excess is beyond me. I still can't believe how selfish and inconsiderate I was." Sadie shook her head.

"Water under bridges," mumbled Ivy as she slipped the green gown over her head. "Oh, this is lovely. And perfect for church on Easter Sunday."

"I've a hat to match it here somewhere," added Sadie, digging through the pile of clothing.

Ivy waited for Sadie to locate the hat, unable to believe the change in her friend. She'd become a totally different person after everything she'd endured. Ivy loved her like a sister. And then Ivy's heart almost stopped.

"Do you still do all the banking for the Circle M Ranch?" she whispered.

Sadie glanced over her shoulder. "Yes. Why would you ask that out of the blue?"

Ivy swallowed hard. Out of the blue indeed. How could she explain her concern? Ivy would never forgive herself if something happened to her friend, especially with her being pregnant. There were no signs of complications so far, and Ivy intended to ensure there remained none. At least, none that she could have prevented.

Ivy thought she might be sick. What if her father and brothers robbed the bank at the exact moment Sadie stood inside depositing funds for the Maxwell ranch? Unthinkable. How could she warn her friend of a possible mishap at the same bank at which Sadie's father had been manager at one time?

"Is it wise to travel all the way to town so often? Couldn't Chance or his brother do the banking until your baby is born?" suggested Ivy. She hoped Sadie didn't detect the desperation she heard in her own voice.

"You're being silly, Ivy," scolded Sadie. "Goodness, like I said, I won't be delivering this baby for a couple of months yet. Perhaps at the end of my eighth month, I'll slow down my work schedule for the final four weeks so I can concentrate on my mothering skills. I've been practicing on my little stepson, you know. He's absolutely adorable, cute as a bug and talks my ears off."

Ivy tugged the lovely dress off over her head. Her stomach threatened to rebel and Ivy suspected her face might match the shade of green perfectly. She should have known Sadie wouldn't heed her subtle warnings, being as stubborn and as independent as Ivy herself.

"Then perhaps one of the ranch hands should accompany you to the bank, just as a precaution in case something should happen," hedged Ivy.

"The Circle M's assistant foreman always accompanies me to town, especially when I have Teddy along with me. Chance insists nothing must happen to me or my stepson." Sadie began hanging the dresses on the corner rack Ivy had rigged up for herself, hating to use the nails sticking out of the wall. She'd hung a few pictures instead.

Ivy blew out her breath. "Well that's wise, and it puts my mind at ease somewhat," she conceded.

"Goodness, you've become such a worrywart. Any heavy lifting is handled by the ranch hand who comes along whenever I shop at the general store. I'm seldom in town more often than once a week, not counting Sunday for church, of course." Sadie straightened and rubbed her lower back with her hands.

"All right, enough." Ivy herded Sadie out of the room and through the classroom to the schoolhouse door. "I cannot thank you enough for your generous gifts. But I'll finish putting everything away myself. And anything I can't fit I'll give to Gertie over at the hotel. She hasn't a lot of wages to spend either."

Sadie hugged Ivy. "An excellent idea, and very generous of you. I adore her twin, Gracie. She's the best sister-in-law a person could ever wish for. She and Cody love each other so much, and with Gracie showing now, they recently made the announcement about an expected baby of their own."

Ivy envied Sadie and Gracie, and she couldn't wait to become a wife and mother, too. But first, her beloved Ernest must propose, and knowing how shy the man could be, months might pass before that happened. And then there would be a wedding to plan. And maybe by sometime next year she'd become his wife. If all the stars were properly aligned. And fate dipped her hand into the mix. Good gravy, Sadie's child could be starting school before Ivy became a bride!

"I'll see you at church on Sunday. Perhaps a little birdy could whisper a hint in Ernest's ear that he should propose to you one of these days." Sadie bobbed her eyebrows.

"Don't you dare!" Ivy wagged her finger at her friend and, despite her impatience, issued a warning. "If Ernest proposes, I insist it be his idea. Something he felt compelled to do, not coerced into by my friend."

Sadie raised her hands in surrender, heading for the door. "All right. I won't say a word. But the man needs to get off his backside and make you his bride."

Ivy playfully crossed her fingers and then waved goodbye to Sadie after she climbed aboard the Maxwell carriage driven by one of the ranch hands. Sighing, Ivy slipped back inside the schoolhouse to choose a pretty dress for her outing with Ernest on Sunday.

* * *

Ernest approached Miles City from the south, having left Spirit Creek before dawn. He'd rested his mount only as necessary, gnawing on hard tack while seated in the saddle instead of stopping to eat. He needed to discuss a number of issues with his counterpart, Sheriff Bob Sanders, and the sooner the better.

Just when he figured he knew what his job was about, something came along and slapped down his confidence a notch. He hadn't any idea how he should proceed with it all, but he'd realized right off that he was in way over his head.

Bob would know what to do.

Ernest dismounted in front of Bob's jailhouse. He hoped his mentor and friend was in town. He'd left in such a rush, he hadn't even thought to send a telegraph to forewarn of his arrival. Damn inconsiderate of him, now that he thought about it. Of course, Bob always assured him that he could ask for assistance with anything, anytime. Ernest was taking him up on the offer today.

"Well, look what the cat dragged in," called Bob Sanders, the second Ernest walked through the door.

Ernest smiled and removed his Stetson. "How-do, Bob."

"What brings you out our way?"

"You might not believe me when I tell you." Ernest shook the other sheriff's hand. "But I need your help with this. I'm pure baffled as to where to ever start."

Sanders poured coffee into a tin mug and handed it to Ernest.

"Come on in, take a chair and tell me what you're yammering about," he said, directing Ernest toward a small office a short ways down the hallway.

Ernest followed him inside and settled on the chair across from the local lawman. "You won't believe what I've just learned. And be damned if I know what to do about it."

Two hours and several mugs of brew later, Ernest strolled out of the Miles City jailhouse. His jumbled thoughts had straightened themselves out under Bob Sanders' tutelage, and he felt prepared to handle the situation he'd found himself thrown into.

Now, for more pleasant matters.

Ernest mounted up and headed off in search of a jewelry merchant with a mail-order catalogue.

CHAPTER 5

Wednesday, April 20, 1892

Ivy quickened her step, rushing toward the hotel to share the noon meal with Pearl Johnson, the doctor's wife, and Agnes Armstrong, the local midwife. The two ladies had suggested meeting to discuss any school-age children that Ivy believed were not receiving adequate nutritional or medical care at home. Or any child requiring a few new clothes from the charitable donation boxes at the church. Elizabeth Waverly agreed to supervise the children's schoolyard playtime during the mid-day break until she returned.

Soon, she lost herself in private thoughts, recalling Easter celebrations when she attended the church service last Sunday, alongside Ernest and his family. Afterwards, the church ladies had organized a special luncheon with games and treats for the children. She'd worn the lovely silk and lace, mint-green hand-me-down from Sadie, and she'd never felt more beautiful. Judging by the admiring looks and broad smile on Ernest's face when he picked her up to walk her to church, her beloved had appreciated the extra care she'd taken in her appearance.

Ivy rounded the corner and strode down the wooden boardwalk. The Sunday outings with Ernest's family became a weekly event, and it was understood that she'd take the noon meal with them at the park or at his parents' home during inclement weather. But she appreciated his thoughtfulness anyway, dropping by the schoolhouse for the specific purpose of asking her to accompany him every week.

She'd so hoped her beloved would have proposed on Easter

Sunday; it would have made the day even more perfect. But he hadn't. She prayed she'd masked her emotions and her disappointment hadn't been obvious to anyone. Perhaps he would ask soon. In the meantime, she'd be living on pins and needles waiting.

Although overwrought with worry as to whether or not Blake truly had left town, she hadn't caught even a glimpse of him for four weeks now, not since he first appeared in Spirit Creek and sent that mysterious telegraph. Perhaps he'd just been passing through like Ernest suspected, and all would be fine. After all, what reason would her father and brothers have to rob an insignificant financial institution like the Spirit Creek Commerce and Trust Bank? Or had she missed something?

Up ahead on the sidewalk outside the bank, a gentleman dressed in an army officer uniform conversed animatedly with the stagecoach driver and Mr. Stafford, the bank manager. Ivy slowed her pace and casually passed by them while eavesdropping on their heated conversation. Another soldier stood nearby, holding a rifle at the ready. For what reason, Ivy wasn't certain. Two other gentlemen stood a ways apart from the others, but their crude clothing suggested they weren't with the army.

"That payroll is destined for our soldiers at Fort Keogh and it will be arriving in about a month." Clearly, the officer appeared in charge of whatever arrangements were being discussed.

Ivy had heard that the soldiers' fort was located somewhere west and south of Miles City, placing it an hour or so ride to the northwest of Spirit Creek.

"I can assure you, Lieutenant, your shipment will be safe in my bank until distributed to your men," insisted Mr. Stafford. "The funds will be locked in the vault at all times. It couldn't be more secure."

"I would expect nothing less of you," growled the officer.

"We'll be prepared for its arrival. Nothing will happen to those monies," reiterated Stafford.

Ivy's heart almost stopped. That was it! The army payroll. The reason her father and brother intended to rob the bank. All of it made sense to her now. But how dare they? No doubt those soldiers worked extremely hard for every penny they earned. And her family had decided to just help themselves to those fellows' wages. Well, she wouldn't stand for it.

But what could she do?

She continued on toward the hotel, knowing it would be difficult to eat lunch, sip tea, and discuss the well-being of the community's less fortunate children. But she'd do it for her students. And then she'd head back to the schoolhouse and complete the day's work.

Tonight, however, she must formulate a plan to sabotage her family's intentions. Her father and brothers could have been planning this robbery for months. She had a mere four weeks to ensure it never happened.

Friday, April 22, 1892

Blake awoke, scratched the stubble itching his face, and crawled out of his bedroll. He stretched his back and glanced at the sun slowly peeking out from the horizon. With his bladder threatening to explode, he watered a cottonwood tree on his way to the horses' makeshift corral. After buttoning his denims, he checked on Humbug and fed him some oats.

Ten minutes later, he returned to the campsite, accepting the tin mug of steaming coffee his father offered.

"Morning, Pa." He took a sip. At least his father could brew a half-decent cup of morning wake-up, unlike that damn cook he had tagging along with them.

"Set yerself down, son." Charlie Connors settled himself on a downed log and poked at the fire.

"Something on your mind?" Blake took a spot alongside him.

"I bin meanin' to ask ya about an old buddy of mine. Jimmy George Barkley. Also used another name when he robbed banks and trains in Californie, but dang if this old brain can remember what it was. Don't really matter none. I heard he got hisself kilt somewhere around these parts." Charlie sipped his coffee.

Blake met his father's eyes. "What point are you trying to make?"

"Just figured someone mighta mentioned him when ya was talkin' to folks."

Blake had heard all about Jimmy George Barkley during the course of his travels. Ornery cuss and dishonest to the core. Mean streak as wide as the state of Texas. Why would anyone in Spirit Creek make mention of someone they had probably long forgotten. And with good reason. "Nobody mentioned anyone by that name," said Blake, hoping his pa would drop the matter.

Charlie nodded. "Guess ya weren't in town all that long, now that I think on it."

"I tried to lay low and not make a lot of inquiries, raise any suspicions." Blake's stomach growled hinting to him that some eggs and bacon would be welcome.

"Makes sense."

Blake rose. "I'm going to see if that cook has some vittles ready."

"His name's Marvin. Good man with explosives as well as a frying pan. Could knock the balls off a bumblebee with a stick of dynamite," cackled Charlie.

With that nonsensical statement, Blake realized not much his pa said these days even made sense. Castrate a bee with dynamite? His pa's memory seemed shot to hell as well. Blake would suggest the old man should see a doctor, but that would be a total waste of time. Best let him be. Blake knew Albert would always watch over their pa.

Unless clearing land for a new enterprise, all legal and above board, Blake hadn't much use for fellows who dynamited things for personal gain or entertainment. "I'll talk to you later, Pa." Blake walked away, still feeling somewhat sympathetic toward the bee.

Charlie rose and lumbered along behind Blake. "We're not finished, son. We need to finalize these plans, determine every move to the second. Ain't riskin' anything goin' wrong. This job is too dang important."

Blake heaved a heavy sigh. They'd gone over the damn plan dozens of times. If able to talk, Humbug could recite the plan! Over a plate of flapjacks, bacon and eggs, Blake and his family once again reviewed what his pa considered a foolproof plan to steal the army payroll from the local bank.

"Since I'm in charge of this outfit, I'll be goin' into town from now on," announced Charlie.

"Hell no, Pa," piped up Albert.

"What ya mean by…"

"Think on it, Pa." Albert cut off his father's objection. "Yer picture could be hung on a wall in the jailhouse. If that sheriff or deputy or anyone else in town recognizes you, that puts an end to our plans. With you locked in a jail cell, how's Blake and me gonna steal that money by ourselves? Ya know old Marvin ain't gonna be no help."

Charlie scratched his scruffy salt-and-pepper beard. "Guess ya got a point there."

"You bet I do."

"I am gettin' rather famous," boasted Charlie, beaming. "Well, I figure ya best go to town next time, Albert. Can't have Blake returnin' there. Should only take one more trip to check on matters a'fore we steal that money."

Albert grinned. "I can sneak into town and poke around a bit, ask a few questions. Just say I'm passin' through and needed some grub, maybe buy a couple bottles of whiskey at a saloon and then disappear before anyone starts gettin' suspicious."

"Yep. Makes sense," agreed Charlie. "Think up a reason why ya need to get inside that bank. We need to know how many ways in and out of the place there are. Get a head count of the fellers workin' there also."

"I'll pretend I'm waitin' for some money to be transferred, make inquiries and tell them I must have made a mistake. Got the name of the town wrong. Then I'll skedaddle," hooted Albert.

"Absolutely genius, brother," offered Blake in an effort to keep up the charade. "Avoid The Spirit Creek Hotel though." *And a pretty waitress named Gertie.* "I noticed that the local lawmen like to take some of their meals there."

"Thanks, Blake. I'll remember that." Albert slapped him on the back.

Blake grimaced. The brotherly affection had been carried out with a little more force and enthusiasm than appeared called for, but enduring a little pain seemed worth it to ensure his mangy sibling avoided running into Gertie.

"I'll let ya know when I want ya to go into town, son," stated Charlie, settling the matter.

CHAPTER 6

Friday, April 29, 1892

When Ivy first arrived in Spirit Creek, she'd explained away the frequent correspondence from her beloved aunt as letters from a girlfriend from normal school who, although they weren't related, shared the same surname. The ruse worked perfectly. Until now.

Ivy stood on the boardwalk outside the general store, squinting in the blinding sunlight as she read the letter she received this morning from Aunt Minnie in California. For the third time. Unfortunately, the words hadn't changed with each repeated reading.

The two-page missive informed Ivy that her beloved aunt decided to venture out for a much-overdue visit. At fifty-six, her aunt rationalized that she wasn't getting any younger. If she intended to see Montana and the niece she hadn't seen in more than two years and loved like a daughter, it had better be now or never. The letter was dated almost three weeks ago.

Ivy's hand flew to her mouth.

Her aunt was surely already on the way!

"No, no, no," muttered Ivy. This couldn't be happening. She couldn't believe her aunt's poor timing.

In the letter, Aunt Minnie had promised to send a telegram a few days before her impending arrival to ensure Ivy met her at the stagecoach. Her aunt signed off exclaiming how she couldn't wait to see her niece in person. Ivy wished she shared her aunt's sentiments, but the inevitable visit had disaster written all over it. She silently chastised herself for that last uncharitable thought, but her aunt couldn't have chosen a more inopportune time to come.

Ivy suspected there was no possible way to track down her aunt en route and insist she turn back and return home. And what possible reason could she offer that would seem feasible to her aunt? Nothing short of an outbreak of bubonic plague would deter her lovable but stubborn aunt once her decision had been made. *Sorry, Auntie, but Pa and my brothers plan to rob the bank. Please delay your visit* wasn't going to deter Aunt Minnie one iota.

"Good morning, Miss Patterson," greeted the banker's wife as she approached.

Ivy's head whipped up. "Um… good morning, Mrs. Stafford."

"Are you feeling all right? You're so pale." She reached for Ivy's hand, noticing the letter she held. "Was it bad news? A death? Is there anything I can do?"

"No, no, nothing like that." Ivy smiled to reassure the kind woman. "I'm just a little surprised by something my friend included in her letter. I'm fine."

"I'm relieved to hear it's nothing serious. I'll carry on with my shopping." Mrs. Stafford scurried inside the store.

"See you at church on Sunday," called Ivy.

She headed toward the telegraph office to send her aunt's neighbor a telegram. The best scenario would be a reply that her aunt's departure has been delayed and Ivy wasn't too late to stop her. Just a foolish wish, that.

At the very least, Ivy needed to know the specific date her aunt left Sandy Point in hopes of better estimating the date of her arrival in Spirit Creek. *Sandy Point.* As she approached the telegraph office building, Ivy experienced a brief moment of nostalgia, recalling the many happy memories of her home town that she cherished and tucked away in her heart. So small, if you blinked as you rode through the community of Sandy Point, California, you'd miss it completely. But the people cared for each other and watched out for their neighbor's well-being as much as their own. Strangers were spotted in a minute, and the crime rate was nonexistent. The drunken sheriff caused more kafuffles at the local watering hole than anyone else. Ivy would have returned in a heartbeat had she been hired to teach, but the same spinster schoolteacher who'd taught her still remained employed there.

Ivy dragged open the telegraph office's heavy wooden door and stepped inside. She prayed her aunt had been waylaid in her plans. What if her aunt arrived and encountered her brother returning to town? Or worse yet her father? What if the matron blew the whistle on Ivy's true identity? How would Ivy explain her lies to Ernest? Or to his family whom she'd come to love as her own? Biting her lip, she realized this entire situation had progressed from bad to worse.

"Hello, miss," greeted the old telegraph operator.

"I need to send an urgent telegraph, please." Ivy dug in her reticule for her change purse.

* * *

Blake couldn't believe his ears. His pa now intended to just waltz into the bank and rob it of the army payroll. In broad damn daylight.

"That idea is the dumbest, most daft thing I've ever heard," he blurted.

Charlie scowled, unaccustomed to anyone questioning his decisions.

"I thought we were robbing the bank in the wee hours of the night." Blake sighed.

"Well, son, we ain't got no dynamite. Marvin said he'd arranged it, but it ain't here yet. How the hell ya figure we can blow up a locked vault with no dynamite?"

Blake considered his pa's reasoning. The old man had a point. Blake figured they'd be doing the job when there was no one around, ensuring no innocent bystanders got hurt. This hiccup in their planning created a new problem for Blake. In light of this change, he needed to send a telegraph to his old pal, Clayton.

"Dynamite," scoffed Blake. Dangerous stuff at the best of times. But in the hands of someone like Charlie Connors or this Marvin fellow, the possible outcomes didn't warrant consideration. He silently thanked the heavens that his father hadn't acquired any.

"So, we dash into the bank, grab the money out of the vault, and run for the hills," summarized Blake.

"Exactly. Although I figure we'll head for Mexico. Ain't certain they got many hills there. A'course I ain't never been there a'fore, so maybe they does." Charlie picked his teeth with a matchstick.

Blake shook his head. Maybe he'd been adopted and his mother just never mentioned it.

"And we ain't got nuff time to get us another order of dynamite, so we gotta do it without," spat Albert.

Blake tipped his head heavenward. *Thank you for small mercies.*

"The element of surprise is our best bet then," reasoned Blake.

"Yep. Bank fellers won't know what hit 'em. We grab the loot and skedaddle. They still be scratchin' their asses wonderin' what happened," cackled Charlie, slapping his knee.

Blake straightened. "So, the payroll is scheduled to arrive in town on Wednesday, May 11th. At least, that's the rumblings I've heard from reliable sources. When do you intend to rob the bank?"

"Near as I figure…"

Oh, Lord, thought Blake. Experience told him nothing good ever came of his pa's figuring. "Repeat what you just said, Pa. I think I might have missed some of it," requested Blake.

"Well, dammit, keep your ears open," scolded Charlie. "I said near as I figure, the army will be handin' out that money a few days after it gets delivered. Probably by the 15th."

"All right, I'm with you so far." Blake noticed his older brother nodding in agreement.

"So we steal it first thing Friday morning a'fore they gets a chance to give it to them soldier fellers."

Blake checked his mental calendar. That would put the robbery date as Friday, May the thirteenth. His pa never attended church a day in his life, far as he knew. He doubted his father even realized number 13 was considered unlucky because there were 13 people, Christ and the 12 Apostles, present at the Last Supper. Blake smiled at the irony. All right then, Friday the thirteenth it was.

Now, he could put his own plan in motion.

* * *

Ernest felt plumb hornswoggled as to what was troubling Ivy. He strode down the sidewalk heading straight for her, but she appeared so deep in thought she didn't even notice him approaching. Had their relationship faltered to the point he'd become invisible to her?

"Good afternoon, Ivy," he began, but his voice croaked. His mouth was as dry as rangeland dust during an August drought.

Her head whipped up and she met his eyes.

He swallowed hard. What if she brushed him off? Offered a lame excuse for hurrying onward? Too busy to spend even a minute of her time in pleasant conversation with the man she claimed to love?

Ivy smiled broadly. "Ernest! Goodness, it's lovely to run into you like this. I was just thinking about you."

Ernest blew out his breath and removed his hat. He reached for her hand and kissed the back of it. She'd been thinking about him. That was a good thing. Unless she was practicing her words, deciding how to end their courtship.

"I'm hoping you'll tell me what's got you so troubled. You seem more twisted up than a ball of Ma's yarn after the cat's been at it."

Ivy shook her head. "It's nothing really."

He didn't believe a word of it.

"You'd tell me if it was serious? I'd like to help, sweetheart. Please, you know you can tell me anything." Ernest placed her hand over his heart. "It pains me something awful to know that your mind's not at peace."

Tears welled in her eyes, and he hoped he'd gotten through to her. Prayed she'd share whatever was bothering her. He couldn't love her more, and when he saw the turmoil in her eyes it nearly ripped his heart right out of his chest.

"Don't concern yourself, Ernest. I'll be fine." She patted his cheek while blinking her tears away. "You're such a dear man for worrying about me."

Ernest covered her hand with one of his own. His greatest fear, that she'd found another man to care for, niggled at his mind. Surely, if another man had caught her eye she would make a clean break of it. Or was she still holding out hope that he'd propose to her before long? Desperate situations called for immediate action, and that's exactly what he intended to do. Lord knows, the situation couldn't appear more desperate. "I'd best get back to work. I was just heading down to the bank to deposit some funds and then I should check out the saloons before heading back to my office. With so many drifters passing through, even in the afternoons there are a few fisticuffs over a card game or a similar wager."

Ivy patted his arm. "Be careful, sweetheart. Don't trust any of those drifters or other ruffians that patronize those saloons. You never know what any of them is capable of doing."

"I'll be wary. Don't worry about me." He dared to kiss her cheek and then, blushing prettily, she headed off down the street in the direction of the hotel.

Probably meeting one of her lady friends for afternoon tea, he speculated, savoring the endearment she'd offered with her warning. He could see in her eyes that something serious had her insides tied up in knots, however. And he had absolutely no idea what it might be. Until they'd spoken the 'I do's' and she became his forever, he couldn't rest easy.

Saturday, April 30, 1892

Ivy strode through her classroom and opened the schoolhouse door, half expecting to find Sadie on her doorstep. She caught her breath, discovering the sickly old telegraph operator standing there and preparing to knock again.

"Goodness, have you received a reply?" she blurted.

The old fellow had resembled a skeleton since the day she arrived in town, and she marveled at how he remained alive. He handed her a piece of paper. "No, miss. This is for you, from another party."

Ivy grimaced, knowing exactly who had sent the message. *Aunt Minnie.*

"Thank you for delivering this in person. I appreciate it. Wait here a moment, please." Ivy scurried to her living quarters and wrapped a half dozen cookies in a clean rag before returning to the doorway. "Here you go. A little something for your thoughtfulness."

"Shucks, miss. I deliver telegrams all the time. No need to pay me nothin' for it," he offered, while accepting her little package nonetheless.

"I insist. You enjoy those cookies." Ivy knew it would take a lot more than six cookies to put some fat on him, but it was a start.

The old fellow headed for the schoolyard gate and glanced back over his shoulder. "Thank you, miss. I surely do appreciate this."

"Goodbye," she called as she closed the door.

Ivy returned to the back and slumped onto a kitchen chair. She took a deep breath and unfolded the paper.

Arriving Wednesday Stop.

Ivy smiled. No one would ever accuse her aunt of frivolous spending. But those simple words told her everything she needed to know. On May 4, her aunt would arrive in Spirit Creek and Ivy's entire world could crash down around her four days from now.

Ivy gasped aloud. She had no way of knowing when the army payroll was scheduled to arrive. What if the payroll was traveling on the same stagecoach as her aunt? What if her suspicions were wrong? What if her father and brother intended to steal the money before it ever reached the bank? What if they'd planned to rob the stagecoach? What if gunfire erupted?

Her aunt's life could be in jeopardy!

When had everything become so complicated? And all due to a fib about her past and her lack of family. The universe had decided to repay that little white lie by possibly placing her beloved aunt in harm's way and by ruining all hopes of her living a happy life with the man she loved.

Why had she done it?

She should have just owned up to the fact that she came from a crate of bad apples. She should have let her friends and acquaintances decide for themselves whether or not to accept her into their community of law-abiding, hard-working folks. Too late now for should haves.

The biggest should have of all…she should have told Ernest about all of it long before now.

Was it too late?

If only she knew what to do!

CHAPTER 7

Monday, May 2, 1892

Ivy accepted the fact that her aunt would arrive in two days. She dismissed her students after final class and promptly headed to the general store to restock her food supplies in anticipation of entertaining her aunt for a meal or two.

Since Aunt Minnie couldn't be expected to stay with her in her small living quarters, Ivy had reserved a room at The Spirit Creek Hotel for two weeks, warning June Davidson that her visitor could very well delay the departure for home. June agreed not to rent the room until she knew the guest wouldn't require it. Fortunately, June hadn't asked any questions about the patron.

Ivy turned the corner and strode down the wooden boardwalk, her list clenched in her hand. She gazed across the street and tripped on a loose board, catching her balance at the last moment before she landed spread-eagled on the sidewalk. She gasped and dropped her list as her hand flew to her mouth. Her oldest brother, Albert, rode down the street on his sway-backed horse, turning at the corner and heading toward the district in town that proper ladies never acknowledged: the area of Spirit Creek that housed the saloons and whorehouses.

Albert hadn't changed a bit. Same scowl on his face and shabby appearance, and still riding the familiar worse-for-wear horse. That poor animal must be twenty years old, at least. She would have thought the critter would have passed by now just to spite its owner, if not to save itself from further abuse.

Ivy bent down and grabbed her list before it blew away in the gentle breeze.

What did her brother's presence in town mean? Where was Blake? And her father? The three of them had to be holed up nearby plotting goodness knows what. Lordy, why had she been born into this family?

Twenty minutes later, she arrived back home and put her purchases away. There wasn't any doubt in her mind that either the stagecoach or the bank would be robbed of that payroll. And, unfortunately, she knew exactly who'd be doing the robbing.

She must warn Ernest!

No avoiding it. If her beloved questioned how she knew about this, she'd just confess all. Her real name and where she hailed from. How she'd escaped. She would tell him about her aunt and using a new name. She wasn't even certain if that was legal, but she'd fess up to it anyway.

She covered her mouth with her hand, forcing down the bile that rose to her throat.

Could she do it? Could she confess everything to Ernest? Knowing it would mean the end to their courtship, to their friendship, to everything in the world she held dear?

She hadn't a choice. She needed to keep her aunt and everyone else in the community she'd come to love safe from danger. Especially Ernest. She couldn't have him blundering into a robbery in progress with no idea how dangerous those responsible were.

She could do this.

At least, she hoped she could. After all, Ernest hadn't proclaimed his undying love for her by proposing. Maybe his feelings for her didn't run as deeply as hers for him. When she thought about it, perhaps she had very little to lose after all.

Wednesday, May 4, 1892

Ivy had asked for the afternoon off for personal reasons, and Mrs. Waverly agreed to teach the remainder of the day in her place. Ivy treated herself to lunch at the hotel and checked that her visitor's room was ready.

Now, she occupied a prominent spot on the boardwalk where she could greet her aunt upon arrival. The stagecoach must be running a bit late. Ivy took a deep breath and blew it out. Only a few other people stood alongside her, waiting for a passenger's arrival or to take delivery of goods of some kind. Ivy wished she was waiting for a box of dry goods instead of her aunt. Cans of beans or bolts of cloth couldn't speak up and give away her secrets.

Ivy heard thundering hooves and the stagecoach's squeaky wheels approaching. She watched the conveyance making its way down the middle of the dusty, rutted street before slowly pulling up to the boardwalk beside the general store.

"Whoa!" yelled the stagecoach driver, pulling on the reins. The horses blew and stood sedately with heads hanging low, obviously quite tired from their journey. The driver set the brake and jumped down from his seat.

Ivy craned her neck for the first glimpse of her aunt. Perhaps she'd been tardy and missed her ride. And then she smiled. Not her aunt. She'd never been late for anything in her life.

The driver settled a wooden step beside the door and yanked it open. "Spirit Creek," he announced.

A tall fellow stepped out first and hurried over to greet a young lady, swinging her up into his arms. Unless the woman was his wife, to some folks the public display might appear unseemly. Ivy only saw two people in love.

"Thank you very much."

Ivy returned her attention to the open doorway, having recognized the voice immediately. Miss Minnie Patterson stepped down from the stagecoach with the driver's assistance. Clasping his proffered hand, she managed the manoeuver with the grace of royalty and the agility of a much younger person. Ivy's heart skipped a beat. How could she ever have wished her aunt would remain at home? She hadn't seen her in over two years and Ivy's eyes filled with tears at the sight of the dear woman.

"Auntie," she whispered.

A slightly-graying head whipped around and a broad smile creased her dear aunt's face. "My, you're a sight for these old eyes of mine. Come here and give me a hug!"

Ivy flew into her aunt's warm and welcoming embrace. The same arms that had held her as she struggled through so many disappointments and hardships while growing up. Had her aunt not taken her in that rainy afternoon when Ivy arrived on her doorstep, looking more like a drowned cat than a twelve-year-old girl, where would she be today? "I can't believe you're really here," she whispered.

Her aunt's robust laugh reminded Ivy of old times when they shared an amusing moment together. "Neither can I, girl. I traveled quite comfortably by train most of the way, but the Deadwood Stage from Miles City leaves much to be desired as a mode of transportation. That hard seat and those creaky wheels brought me to you, however, and for that I would endure almost anything."

Ivy grimaced, recalling her own horrendous trip here when she first accepted the position of schoolteacher. "Seems the journey hasn't improved since I came. But being that the stagecoach is the only offering from Miles City once you leave the train, neither of us had any choice in the matter. Let's get you registered at the hotel. I've reserved a room for you, and I hope you'll be comfortable."

"I won't be staying with you, dear?"

Ivy burst into laughter. "My teacher's quarters are so small, I'd have to suspend you from the ceiling for you to lie down to sleep."

Aunt Minnie shook her head, appearing delighted to have arrived as well as exhausted from her journey. "Then, show me to the hotel. I believe I could sleep for a week, but only if I wasn't hanging from the rafters."

Just then Luke Carlyle, one of the area's wealthiest ranchers, drove his supply wagon up to the general store. He leapt down and tied the horse's reins to the hitching post.

"Luke, just the fellow we need," called Ronald Waverly from the boardwalk.

"Why's that?" replied Luke, shaking the storekeeper's hand.

"Appears Miss Patterson is acquainted with this lady who just arrived in town. I wonder if you could drive her over to the hotel, bring her trunks and boxes along, too?"

Ivy's heart almost stopped. How much had the store owner heard? Ivy recalled whispering the word 'auntie' at least once. She mentally kicked herself for her carelessness when overcome with emotion at seeing her aunt again.

"Can do. I'll leave this list of supplies Maggie requires, and I'll drop back later to pick them up." Luke handed a slip of paper to Mr. Waverly.

"Looks like your Maggie plans on doing some baking," observed Mr. Waverly, disappearing inside the store.

"That isn't necessary, Mr. Carlyle," blurted Ivy. "Mrs. Davidson will send her fellow over to fetch the luggage later."

"No trouble at all," insisted Luke.

"Would you prefer to walk?" Ivy met her aunt's eyes. Hoping it didn't sound like pleading, she added, "We should. I imagine you've been sitting enough."

Her aunt searched Ivy's eyes for several seconds and must have noticed her concern. Without questioning her niece's motives for suggesting such a thing, her aunt replied, "Oh, yes, please. I couldn't sit for another moment. I do appreciate you bringing my belongings along though, sir."

"I'll leave them at the front desk, ma'am." Luke tipped his hat to them.

"Thank you, Mr. Carlyle." Ivy watched him loading her aunt's items into the back of his wagon with the stage driver's assistance.

Thankfully, Luke didn't appear put off by her failure to introduce him to the person for whom he was doing the favor. Under normal circumstances, Ivy wouldn't even consider such a rude gesture toward one of the citizens. Today's circumstances were anything but normal, however. Perhaps Luke was in a rush since he hadn't introduced himself either.

"Do you care to explain what that was about?" whispered her aunt as they set off down the street.

"Not really." Ivy hooked arms with her aunt and headed in the direction of the hotel.

Fifteen minutes later, Ivy and Aunt Minnie stepped into The Spirit Creek Hotel where June Davidson stood behind the registration desk, anticipating their arrival.

"Land sakes, you look done in, ma'am." June glared at Ivy. "Why on earth would you suggest a walk when you could have ridden along with Luke? Goodness, this poor lady appears ready to drop. My name is June Davidson." She offered the new guest her hand.

Aunt Minnie shook hands with the hotel owner. "Delighted to meet you. My name is…"

"Plenty of time for introductions later," interrupted Ivy. "Let's get you registered and up to your room before you faint from exhaustion."

"Excellent suggestion, Ivy," agreed Mrs. Davidson. "The whole town just adores this wonderful young lady. She's one of the best teachers we've ever employed here."

"Thank you so much for saying that, Mrs. Davidson," exclaimed Ivy.

"Every word the truth."

"I do hope a hot bath and a hot meal aren't too much to ask, Mrs. Davidson?" inquired Aunt Minnie.

"Goodness, no. And being that you know Ivy, call me June." June shoved the hotel register toward her newest guest. "Please sign yourself in and I'll run and order a bath for you right now." June hustled down the hallway and disappeared from sight.

Ivy reached for her aunt's hand, preventing her from putting pen to paper in the large leather-bound register.

"Don't sign your name as Patterson, please," she whispered.

Aunt Minnie stared at her niece as if she'd sprouted a horn atop her head.

"And may I ask why not?"

"It's a long story."

Aunt Minnie sighed. "Ivy, I love you like a daughter. I understood your reasons for using your mother's maiden name, Patterson, but I will not lie for you." She quickly signed the register as Miss Minnie Patterson from Sandy Point, California.

Ivy's eyes filled with tears. How on earth would she explain her aunt to everyone? Perhaps temporary insanity would do. Although she'd been carrying on this farce since the day she herself set foot in Spirit Creek. Hardly temporary. This whole business was slowly driving her crazy. Perhaps permanent insanity would suit better.

June Davidson returned. "Your bath will be prepared within the half hour. I anticipated your request and had a bathtub taken up to your room already. Gertie will be up with hot water and fresh towels in no time. And I'll send up a plate of food at six o'clock." She glanced at the register and read aloud, "Miss Minnie Patterson. Good heavens, are you related to Ivy?"

"She took me in after my mother died," blurted Ivy. And truly, it wasn't a lie. Her aunt did raise her as her own after her mother passed so suddenly. Mrs. Davidson didn't need to know she'd been a twelve-year-old runaway at the time.

"Such a generous thing to do, and her being no relation or anything. Ivy explained that she was an orphan." Mrs. Davidson patted Ivy's hand. "Miss Patterson, you did an exceptional job of raising this foundling and allowing her to use your name. She's a wonderful young lady."

"Isn't she just though," mumbled Aunt Minnie, rolling her eyes. "Thank you for arranging the bath. I can't tell you how much I appreciate your thoughtfulness. And please call me Minnie."

"Ivy, I can take Minnie up to her room and help her get settled in if you have other things that require your attention." June beamed at her newest tenant.

"I appreciate that. I should get back to the school and prepare tomorrow's lessons." Ivy smiled at her aunt. "No wandering around checking out the town. Stay in your room and rest for a few days. You've had a long, tiring journey."

"I must admit I agree with you. But be a dear and please see me to my room, Ivy."

When an argument hadn't been forthcoming, relief washed over Ivy. She wanted her aunt safely tucked away in her room where she wouldn't be running into the likes of Ivy's father or brothers. At least, not until Ivy had the opportunity to explain the situation to her. Meantime, she had to steer her aunt away from public places where she might give away her secrets.

"I'll just see…Minnie up to the room and then I'll say my goodbyes," stated Ivy.

"I'll show you the way. My hired man placed your trunks and things in your room already," said June. "I realized Ivy's guest was female when I spotted those lovely hat boxes."

The three ladies entered the hotel room and Ivy felt her eyes widen. A large four-poster bed covered with a colorful patchwork quilt occupied the center of the room and stood atop a beautiful cream and purple floral rug. Floor length lavender-colored panels covered the twin windows separated by a small fireplace. Two ladder-back chairs kept company at a small round wooden table where a bouquet of lilacs served as a centerpiece atop a white linen tablecloth.

"This room is beautiful," mumbled Ivy, taking it all in.

"Thank you. I reserve it for female customers only. I doubt many male tenants would appreciate it. Soon as I spotted those hat boxes, I knew immediately this room would be perfect for our guest. I'll go see about that hot water." June dashed out the door, leaving Ivy and Minnie alone.

Minnie removed her hat and set it atop the table, all the while her eyes never straying from her niece.

Ivy's face warmed.

"Do you mind explaining why I've suddenly become no better than a glorified guardian?"

Ivy took a deep breath. "I've been living a little white lie since I arrived here."

"And?" encouraged her aunt.

While Ivy attempted to arrange her thoughts and come up with a plausible explanation for what she'd done, Aunt Minnie hiked up her skirts and removed a small derringer and leg holster strapped to her thigh.

Ivy almost swallowed her tongue and gasped. "Aunt Minnie!"

Her aunt hid the holstered weapon under the mattress. "Do you think I survived all these years of spinsterhood by knitting tea cozies and baking pies for church fundraisers? I've encountered more than one fellow who intended to begin a relationship with a wedding night and no mention of I do's. A lady needs to protect herself."

"But with a gun? Certainly you could convince them some other way."

"I've discovered that if I aim my gun at their chest and voice my displeasure, they laugh it off. If I aim at crotch level, they take me, my gun, and my displeasure with them much more seriously." Her aunt settled the bedcovers back into place.

Ivy slumped onto the bed. "Good gravy. I never would have guessed. I'm not certain I should explain myself. You might shoot me for my silliness."

"How foolish are we talking?"

Just then, Gertie knocked on the door and bustled into the room. "Here's your hot water, Miss Patterson. And I've brought you three large towels. If you'd like more, just ask for them." Gertie carried a pail of cold water and June's hired man carried two buckets of steaming hot water.

"Thank you, both of you."

The fellow ducked out of the room without a word, his cheeks flaming, and obviously wanting to be nowhere near the vicinity of a lady or her bath.

"Hi, Ivy, I didn't notice you sitting there." Gertie smiled and then returned her attention to the hotel guest. "Would you like some help with your corsets, Miss Patterson?"

Aunt Minnie waved off the suggestion. "Thank you, but no. Ivy can help me."

Gertie bobbed her head and exited, closing the door behind herself.

Aunt Minnie scoffed, "Corset, my foot. Haven't worn one of the blasted things in years."

Ivy gaped at her aunt. Had she ever really know the woman?

"Don't look so shocked. I couldn't gain weight if you glued a pound to me. If you don't require a corset why bother with the thing?"

Ivy had to agree with her aunt's reasoning, and suddenly wondered why she wore one on her own stick-thin frame?

"Now, you were about to explain some foolishness to me. Help me out of these clothes while you're doing it. My arms feel made of lead and my legs are as wobbly as a newborn deer's." Aunt Minnie yanked pins out of her hair as she spoke.

For the next half hour, Aunt Minnie lounged beneath a sea of bubbles in the steaming rose-scented bath while Ivy explained what she'd done, outlining every scenario of her dilemma.

"Goodness, young lady. A writer of those dime novels couldn't make up something like that. How on earth did you think you'd get away with such a tale?" Aunt Minnie reached for her hand and Ivy fought the urge to burst into tears. "I do understand why you did it though. And I can't fault you for wanting to put those dreadful men out of your life. It's the reason you came to me in the first place. But to lie about having no family… Why, that includes me, too."

"I know. And I'm so sorry. I realized the corner I'd backed myself into when your first letter arrived over a year ago, so I explained it away as correspondence from a friend with the same surname although no relation to me."

Aunt Minnie tittered, "You always were able to think on your feet."

"*Lie* on my feet is more like it." Ivy brushed at a tear. There'd be no feeling sorry for herself. It was her own fault she'd fallen into this predicament.

"Well, until you find the opportunity to explain all this to your sheriff, I'll keep mum about how we're related. But you will tell him everything, Ivy, and as soon as possible. Now scoot, so I can finish my bath and get my nightgown and wrapper on before that lovely young girl bustles in here with my supper."

Ivy kissed her aunt's cheek, half expecting her to pull her into the tub as a joke. After seeing that little gun, nothing would surprise her. "Thank you for keeping my secret. I'm going to see Ernest right now, and I'll confess everything."

Ivy headed downstairs on her way to the jailhouse to confront Ernest. So far she'd confessed to the lies she'd told the townsfolk. But Ivy hadn't warned her aunt that she suspected Charlie Connors and her brothers were hiding out close by and planned to rob the darn bank!

Her aunt had only just arrived safe and sound, and Ivy couldn't ruin her first night with such distressing news. Tomorrow or the next day would be plenty of time to fill her aunt in on the rest of it. After she'd explained it all to Ernest.

CHAPTER 8

Ivy mustered up her courage while she strode north toward the jailhouse. The square-shaped, wood-and-brick building had been built a little ways away from the seedier part of town, but close enough for the sheriff or deputy to respond to pleas for help whenever a ruckus broke out in one of the saloons or whorehouses.

A light burned in the only window facing the street. Ernest hadn't left for the small house he and his brother rented from Luke Carlyle. She took a deep breath, opened the door, and peered inside.

"How-do, Miss Patterson," greeted Deputy Donald Jones, sitting tipped back in the sheriff's chair, boots planted atop his brother's desk. Tossing aside the dime novel he'd been reading, he moved his boots and stood. "Is there trouble in town? Something I can help you with?"

"No, nothing's wrong." Ivy crept across the threshold and closed the door behind her. "But I must speak to Ernest immediately."

Donald scratched his head. "Well, that's going to be a bit of a problem, I'm afraid. Ernest left for Miles City early this morning. Going to be staying overnight for sure, and maybe another day as well."

"What!" Ivy's hand flew to her mouth.

Goodness sakes! Ernest had left the town unprotected, except for his brother, a novice deputy. This wasn't good at all. Not one little bit. What if her family chose tonight to break into the bank and rob it? She took a deep breath, sighed in relief. No, that wouldn't happen. The army shipment hadn't arrived yet.

"Well, Miss Patterson, tell you the truth, I'm surprised he didn't mention it to you so you wouldn't worry or nothing." Donald stood hands on hips. "Of course, I don't expect there'll be much happening. Maybe a few fisticuffs if the outcome in a poker game goes wrong in some feller's estimation. But I don't expect anything I can't handle."

Ivy wrung her hands. "I suppose not," she conceded. She couldn't very well blurt out her concerns without giving away her secret, or without as likely as not giving Donald heart palpitations. She didn't suppose him capable of dealing with a gang of bank robbers on his own, and she expected neither did he. Ernest must return as soon as possible. He just had to.

"Don't you fret none, ma'am. Ernest told me he's working on some case with that Miles City lawman, Sheriff Bob Sanders. But he'll be home just as soon as he can. I'm certain of it." Donald touched her arm, led her toward the door. "I bet he won't be away any later than Saturday. Wouldn't miss spending Sunday afternoon with you, as usual."

"I hope not."

"Gosh, Miss Patterson. You must really love my brother. Can't bear to be away from him for more than a day." Donald shook his head. "I truly do hope I find me a girl who loves me that much some day."

Ivy felt herself blush clear to her hairline.

Donald paled. "Dang it all, I've gone and embarrassed you. I can't believe I said all that out loud. I should learn to think before my lips start flapping. Please accept my apology."

"You're forgiven, Donald." Ivy clasped her reticule with white-knuckled fingers. "I pray Ernest will return safe and sound just as soon as possible."

"I'll tell him to drop by the schoolhouse the minute he sets foot back in town, ma'am."

"Thank you. I'd appreciate that." Ivy turned to leave. And then she glanced over her shoulder. "You take care now and watch your back while you're in charge."

"Will do, ma'am." Donald reached around and opened the door for her. "Ernest deputized Mayor Barker and Ronald Waverly, just as a precaution of course, before he left. So, don't you be worrying. We'll all be fine until my brother comes home."

"I'm certain you're right." Ivy turned and scooted out the door, not believing a word of it. She just prayed nothing would happen until Ernest returned.

She heard the door close behind her.

Ivy hadn't realized the time until she left the jailhouse and noticed that night had settled into Spirit Creek. For a brief moment, she contemplated asking Donald to accompany her home. Shaking her head, she thought it better to leave him free to handle any request for his assistance by the townsfolk.

A cool breeze rustled the leaves overhead on a row of cottonwood trees as Ivy hurried along Second Street, her boots tapping out a steady staccato rhythm on the boardwalk. An owl hooted from a high branch and she startled as she rounded the corner. A man dressed all in black appeared from nowhere and stepped out in front of her. She screamed and her heart leapt into her throat. She'd never come so close to wetting herself since age three!

"Ma'am," he said, softly.

Ivy straightened her spine and stood a little taller, hoping the man didn't notice her fear. Surprisingly, Ivy hadn't detected a liquor stench on his breath when he spoke. At least, he wasn't drunk.

His shabby appearance left no doubt in her mind that he was a penniless drifter. The rags she used to clean the schoolhouse were in better shape than his clothing. In the dim moonlight, she couldn't distinguish any identifying facial features like a scar. His scruffy beard might house any number of infestations though. Dirty, stringy hair peeked out from below his dusty, badly-misshaped hat.

Suddenly, he grabbed her by the shoulders and two strong hands squeezed her upper arms. She nearly swooned with fear of what would inevitably happen next racing through her mind. Every woman's worst nightmare. She prepared to defend herself; she wouldn't be violated by this stranger without a fight.

"I'm Clayton." He met her eyes. "You shouldn't be out alone this late at night. The streets are no place for a decent young lady like yourself."

For a moment, Ivy just stared back, unable to comprehend the kindness she saw in his eyes considering the somewhat rough way he'd handled her.

"I…I was just heading home," she stammered.

He released his grip on her arms and waved her on the way. "Get to it then."

Ivy turned on her heel, hoisted her skirts, and ran, refusing to look behind her. Although, she hadn't heard footsteps following her she wasn't taking any chances. She dashed through the schoolyard gate, flew up the steps and slipped through the doorway. She even slid the wooden bar into place, preventing anyone from barging inside. Something she'd seldom done in this small, friendly town. Had the fellow followed her? Before lighting a lamp, she peeked out through a pane in one of the schoolhouse windows but she couldn't see anyone on the moonlit street.

When she stopped shaking, Ivy quickly prepared for bed. She lay awake in the dark for hours, however, her mind racing with unanswered questions. Why were so many strangers suddenly appearing in Spirit Creek? Usually she never encountered a soul she didn't know. For an instant, she considered it possible that the drifter she encountered robbed banks with her father and brothers. Her family used to operate alone, but that could have changed. Or was he a notorious criminal, intent on doing someone harm? A hired gun?

Every creak and groan in the old building had her jumping. She hated to admit how badly he'd frightened her, despite the bravery she'd shown at the time. She despised living this way. Questioning people's motives. Frightened by someone she encountered on the street at night. Or was she just being silly? Probably, the fellow had found himself down on his luck, an unemployed cowhand who'd come searching for work on one of the area ranches. At least, she hoped so.

"Ivy, you're just letting your fertile imagination run amuck. Now settle down and go to sleep!" she chastised herself.

She tossed and turned. Fluffed her feather pillow. Stared at the ceiling barely discernable in the sliver of moonlight coming through her window. She flipped onto her stomach. Still sleep continued to elude her most of the night. She needed to confess her secrets to Ernest and tell him what she knew. Perhaps then her mind would be at peace.

Sunday, May 8, 1892

Ernest almost crawled out of his own skin, sitting in church beside Ivy throughout what seemed the longest sermon in the history of Reverend Gerald's career. Next, Ernest caught his leg bobbing up and down like a duck riding the waves on a pond on a windy day. He'd stilled himself, glancing at Ivy to check if she'd detected his nervousness. She stared straight ahead, appearing enthralled by today's services.

Ernest's spirits had risen when Donald told him how worried Ivy had appeared when she dropped around to see him at the jailhouse while he was away in Miles City. Knowing she cared so much warmed his heart. He couldn't love her more either. The trip couldn't be avoided, however, and Ernest had accomplished a lot during his visit with Bob Sanders.

The Miles City sheriff had taken him under his wing when Mayor Barker had first given him the job of Spirit Creek's new sheriff. Being a former Texas Ranger, Sanders' vast knowledge of law enforcement never ceased to amaze Ernest. He couldn't have asked for a better teacher. And Bob frequently praised Ernest, telling him he was a quick study and how proud he was of him. Ernest had longed to become a Pinkerton detective at one time, but now he was prepared to live out his years as a local sheriff since it meant spending the rest of his life with a wonderful girl like Ivy. A wife and family and a job he loved. What more could a man ask for in life?

Everyone headed outside after the service, moving as slow as a herd of obstinate Longhorns on a cattle drive. Ernest gritted his teeth. The entire world seemed to creep along like a gimped-legged snail today.

A half hour later, Ernest and Ivy arrived at the south end of Grayson Gardens Park. Ernest reached for her hand. "Let's go for a walk. I need to talk to you before Ma sets out the noon meal and we get caught up in conversation with the family."

"I have something I need to tell you, too." Her hand moved to her chest.

Ernest frowned. "Are you feeling all right? If you're ill, sweetheart, I'll take you home immediately."

Ivy shook her head. "No, I'll be fine once we talk."

"I hope so," muttered Ernest, leading Ivy down a stone pathway that ran alongside the creek.

Soon they arrived at their favorite partially secluded area surrounded by towering evergreen trees. Ernest seated her on the bench the town built and paid for to honor Sarah Grayson, the long-time citizen for whom the park had been named. If he remembered correctly, Sarah moved to Philadelphia to be closer to her sister shortly after Ivy arrived in town.

The entire park was maintained through the citizens' volunteer time and attention. Ivy leaned over the end of the bench and, from habit, plucked a weed out of one of the semicircular flower beds. As well as his beloved, a good number of townsfolk developed a green thumb due to the community project. The intoxicating scent of the perennials' blooms filled the air and he watched as Ivy breathed deeply while brushing a bit of dust off her hands. For some reason, she appeared as nervous as he was. Did she suspect what was coming?

"Let me go first, please." He couldn't contain himself another minute.

"All right," agreed Ivy, settling her skirts around her and clasping her hands in her lap.

"Do you remember this spot? Before the flowerbeds were planted or this bench was built? This is the place where I first kissed your cheek." Ernest settled himself on the edge of the bench. "I feared I might faint from nerves," he admitted, smiling.

"Me, too," confessed Ivy.

"I admire you so much and I'm so thankful you can tolerate my energetic and noisy family so well. You know I'm not one for flowery words. When I have something to say, I just say it. Ivy, you mean the world to me, and I love you more than I thought it possible to love another person." He cleared his throat and slid off the bench, situating himself on one knee. "I'd like nothing better than to spend the rest of my days with you, and I'm hoping you feel the same way. Would you do me the honor of becoming my wife?"

Ivy burst into tears.

"Did I say something wrong?" blurted Ernest, feeling himself pale.

"Not at all. It's just…I love you so much. I want to be your wife more than anything."

Ernest dug a small box out of his pocket and opened the lid, revealing a beautiful ruby ring. "Please say you'll marry me."

"Yes! Oh, yes, Ernest, I'll marry you." Ivy gasped. "And you even bought me a ring."

Ernest felt himself beaming as he slipped the ring on her slim finger. It fit perfectly. It had cost him almost half his savings, but she was worth it. "You've just made me the happiest man in the whole world."

Ivy threw her arms around his neck, almost toppling him over before he caught his balance and stood up bringing her to her feet with him.

"I can hardly believe this is happening."

"I know I've been dragging my feet, but I can't lose you to another man, Ivy. You're the only woman for me." Ernest bent his head down and kissed her warm, welcoming lips. Although she kissed him back, he detected a slight reluctance on her behalf. He even saw some hesitation in her eyes. Something was bothering her still. Did it have anything to do with his proposal?

"What's the matter, Ivy? You're not already married to another feller are you?" he speculated, jokingly.

Ivy smiled and playfully swatted his arm. "Of course not. I'm just overwhelmed by all this. I never expected it today."

Ernest wasn't totally convinced she was being honest with him, but he wouldn't ruin this special day by pressing her for an explanation. He'd leave it alone for now. "Tell me, sweetheart, what did you need to discuss with me?"

* * *

"It wasn't that important. Let's share our wonderful news with your family," suggested Ivy, following Ernest back to the picnic area and to the people she'd come to love so much.

Ivy couldn't catch her breath. She'd just become engaged to the love of her life. She'd waited so long for this day, and now it had come. She'd been so preoccupied all morning with practicing her explanation in her head that she hadn't suspected a thing.

Her explanation.

Goodness, how could she tell Ernest her secrets now? Before, she hadn't much to lose. They were courting, nothing permanent expected, no promises of a commitment spoken. But Ernest's proposal changed everything. If she confessed her secrets and her suspicions about her family robbing the bank, she could lose everything. His respect. His love. He'd no doubt recant his proposal.

Feeling like a coward, she admitted to herself that she just couldn't do it. At least, not yet.

Ernest's family had accepted her without question into their homes and their lives. She'd lose their respect in a heartbeat once they learned the truth. Certainly, she'd lose all possibility of a loving husband and a family of her own. She'd so looked forward to raising children with Ernest, a passel of upstanding citizens like their adoring father, so unlike her own poor excuse for a parent.

But what if something went terribly wrong during the inevitable robbery? What if someone was hurt? What if a lawman was murdered? Or worse, what if her own beloved Ernest was killed? Ivy swallowed hard. Could she live with her selfish decision then?

"Ivy, congratulations! The ring is beautiful," exclaimed her future mother-in-law.

Ivy searched Florence Jones' face, seeing nothing but love and happiness in her eyes. "Thank you. I feel so honored to be joining this family."

"We're honored to have you." Earl Jones kissed his future daughter-in-law's cheek.

Ivy's insides churned. But what if she was wrong? What if Blake had been passing through town and nothing more? What if there wouldn't be a bank robbery? Ivy needed time to think and consider all the ramifications of a confession. Surely, waiting a few days wouldn't matter.

Wednesday, May 11, 1892

Ivy stood almost hidden from sight across the street as several boxes labelled 'US Army' were being unloaded from the Deadwood Stagecoach and lugged into the bank under the watchful eye of a half dozen armed soldiers.

The army payroll had arrived.

Ivy couldn't begin to guess exactly how much cash the boxes contained. But judging by the serious expressions on the faces of the soldiers overseeing the unloading, it must be a lot. She almost lost her lunch as trepidation overcame her. What would happen now? How long before her family struck?

There wasn't any choice in the matter. She had to confess everything to Ernest. But how could she do it with so much at stake, personally. Was there some way to warn Ernest without tipping her hand? Without ruining any possible future they could have together?

If only she could be assured her father and brothers intended to strike in the dead of night when no one was around, when no one would be hurt. Could she risk it? But then those poor soldiers would never receive their hard-earned wages.

Why had she ever told the lies in the first place? She should have known the day would come when she'd pay dearly for her deception. And it appeared that day had arrived.

* * *

Hidden on top of the hotel roof, Blake and Albert gazed down the street at the entrance to The Spirit Creek Commerce and Trust Bank some distance away. They watched as the men unloaded the army payroll shipment from the stage and hauled it into the bank.

"Right on time." Albert whistled long and low. "Ain't that the pertiest sight ya ever seen?"

"Pretty indeed," agreed Blake, glancing at his brother who was almost salivating like a dog staring at a juicy steak.

"Ya don't sound very interested," accused Albert, elbowing Blake in the ribs.

Blake swallowed the curse that nearly spilled from his mouth as he inhaled sharply. His brother had surprised him and dang it the jab hurt. Albert's eyes appeared glazed and his voice held the excitement of a child on Christmas morning. Blake reined in his temper. His sibling truly enjoyed stealing what belonged to others, without a hint of remorse. How could they have come from the loins of the same man?

In about forty-eight hours all hell would break loose with Blake dead center of it all. He prayed he just lived through it.

CHAPTER 9

Thursday, May 12, 1892

Aunt Minnie surprised Ivy, dropping by the schoolhouse so late in the evening for a visit, claiming she wanted to enjoy a brisk walk before bed.

Ivy tossed a log into the fire and set the kettle on the woodstove to boil water for tea. She grimaced under her aunt's close scrutiny. Aunt Minnie arrived in Spirit Creek only a little over a week ago, but it seemed like a month.

"You're keeping something from me." Aunt Minnie pursed her lips, taking a seat at the kitchen table. "Don't even try to deny it, girl. You haven't lived under my roof for a while now, but no one knows you like I do."

Ivy busied herself, setting out cups and saucers with the sugar bowl and cream jug. She glanced up and met her aunt's eyes. "I…I…"

"Spit it out. I haven't judged you for fibbing to the entire town about your past. I won't start now. I've even agreed to keep mum for a while because of Ernest's proposal." Her aunt crossed her arms over her bosom.

"I haven't told you everything. But it has nothing to do with the other."

"About lying to the townsfolk. Telling them you're an orphan."

Ivy nodded. "It's worse."

"Good Granny Grady, what else could be so horrible that you're afraid to tell me?" Her aunt shifted forward on her seat.

Ivy smiled at Aunt Minnie's familiar old expression that Ivy hadn't heard in ages and flopped onto the opposite chair. "I observed someone in town a while back. Someone who can only mean trouble, and not just for me."

"Someone?"

"From my past. Someone I prayed would never learn my whereabouts," whispered Ivy.

Her aunt frowned and then she visibly paled. "You don't mean…"

"Blake rode down Main Street like he hadn't a care in the world. Wandered into the hotel and ate lunch." Ivy wrung her hands. "I thought I was hallucinating, even considered the possibility I was mistaken. I hadn't seen him in ten years. But then I heard him laughing at something the waitress said. You know that distinctive laugh of his. It was Blake all right."

"What was he doing here?" Aunt Minnie slumped against the chair back as if someone had knocked the air from her lungs.

"I hadn't a clue at the time. I followed him to the telegraph office and hid outside near an open window. I overheard the old operator read aloud the message Blake sent. I've no idea who the intended recipient was, and the brief message made little sense to me."

"You said *at the time*." Aunt Minnie leaned forward. "Do you know now why he came to Spirit Creek? Have you talked to him?"

Ivy vigorously shook her head. "Heavens, no! I've avoided him completely. But a few weeks later, I almost died of shock when I saw Albert riding his old horse toward the Joker's Wild Saloon."

"Albert is here, too? That can't be a coincidence!" exclaimed her aunt.

Ivy leapt to her feet, hearing the kettle whistle. "Oh, it most certainly isn't. I'd bet my entire new wardrobe that Pa's somewhere nearby. And I'm almost positive the three of them intend to rob the Spirit Creek Commerce and Trust Bank."

Aunt Minnie appeared ready to faint.

"Are you all right, Auntie?" Ivy rushed to her side.

"I'll be fine. Just give me a minute to…to…process all this." Her aunt met her eyes. "Goodness, this means that your father and brothers haven't reformed over the years. They're still criminals, bank robbers. The same scum you escaped from all those years ago."

"I'm afraid you're right." Ivy clasped her aunt's cold hands in hers. "Now, do you see why I told everyone that I'm alone in the world? Why I've kept my past a secret?"

"I suppose so."

"Auntie, I'm almost positive they intend to rob the bank of the army payroll that arrived here yesterday." Ivy strode to the woodstove, grabbing up the kettle to silence the shrill whistle. She poured the boiling water into the teapot and set it on the table. "It makes me so furious when I think of Pa and my brothers just up and stealing those poor soldiers' wages. The three of them have no right to a penny of it."

"You won't get any argument here, girl," whispered her aunt. "But what can we do?"

"Tell everyone the truth," admitted Ivy. "It may cost me everything I hold dear. My reputation in the town. My engagement and marriage to Ernest. His family's affection and respect."

Aunt Minnie exclaimed, "Surely, there's another way! You love that young man so much. And I know he loves you or he wouldn't have proposed."

"I do love him. And that's why I have to fess up to my lies. I need to warn him of the danger. Let him know that the bank will be robbed in a day or two." Ivy poured the tea as she spoke and then set the teapot down. "Auntie, if I thought for a moment I was wrong…"

"You're not wrong, Ivy," stated her aunt, emphatically, sliding forward on her chair. "Don't second guess yourself. Charlie Connors fooled me once. I wouldn't trust him for a minute."

Ivy reared back, surprised by the ferocious words that spewed from her aunt's mouth.

"I didn't mean to frighten you. There's something you don't know, but I suppose you're plenty old enough to learn the truth now." Aunt Minnie met her eyes. "It's the age-old tale of two sisters falling in love with the same man. Charlie loved Rose dearly, barely gave me the time of day. When only age sixteen, Rose voiced her intentions to marry Charlie. Our father encouraged your mother to reconsider, insisting I was four years older and more the marriageable age. But Rose wouldn't hear a word of it."

"You and Pa…"

"Charlie had been courting me openly, but we learned later that he'd been seeing your mother on the sly. I should have guessed. Never once did he so much as kiss my cheek."

Ivy noticed the unshed tears welling in her aunt's eyes. Did she still have feelings for the father Ivy despised? "What happened?"

"Charlie whisked her out of the house in the middle of the night, right from under our father's nose. Charlie and Rose eloped in the next town and then they disappeared. They returned to Sandy Point six months later, with your mother only days away from delivering Albert, her firstborn."

Ivy did the cyphering in her head. "Then that means…"

"Your ma knew she was in the family way when they eloped."

Ivy slumped into the empty chair. "Oh, my goodness."

"I don't harbor any resentment, dear. Don't think for a minute, I regret their union. Until your mother passed so suddenly, she and Charlie enjoyed a happy marriage. Your ma didn't approved of Charlie's robbing and all, but she loved him dearly. She told me so herself. Oh, I miss your mother so much. We remained close, even after she married the man I thought I would love forever."

"I remember my parents arguing late at night when they believed my brothers and I were asleep." Tears burned behind Ivy's eyes, same as had happened when she was a frightened and confused child. For years, she'd thought it her fault that they'd argued. Decided that her parents were unhappy with her, and she'd done everything in her power to please them. But as she aged and understood their words, she'd learned differently. Realized her father's lifestyle had caused their arguments. And lying in bed, she'd silently sided with her mother.

Ivy gaped at her aunt. "And you've never married."

"Never found another man I could love," confided Aunt Minnie, with a sigh. "But once I learned what Charlie had in mind as a means to support his family, I thanked the heavens I'd escaped that life. Unlike your mother, I never would have tolerated it. Likely as not, I would have reported Charlie's whereabouts to the authorities myself."

Ivy laughed. "I've contemplated doing exactly that more times than I can count."

"Charlie has always been trouble. I prayed that your brothers would take after your mother, like you did. But, sadly, it appears those two acorns have taken root under the old tree. Perhaps now is the time to disturb some roots." Aunt Minnie reached for Ivy's hand. "Tell your young man about your family. Admit everything. Surely, he'll understand your reasons for fibbing. Who'd want to admit coming from such sub-standard stock as the Connors clan? Charlie's father wasn't any better. Always had his hand in something illegal, as I recall."

"My brothers willingly followed in Pa's footsteps. I thought perhaps with Blake's love of book-learning, he'd find his way to making a living on the right side of the law. " Ivy sighed heavily. "I guess I'm the only one to take after mother's family."

"And you resemble your dear mother so much, I've nearly called you Rose a couple of times since I arrived," admitted Aunt Minnie, grinning sheepishly.

Ivy gasped, "I do? I keep a much-cherished picture of Ma hidden away in my Bible. She was so beautiful."

"And you're every bit as beautiful, too. Equally hard-working and honest." Her aunt leaned forward and kissed her cheek.

"Except when I'm lying to an entire town of upstanding citizens," bemoaned Ivy.

Aunt Minnie waved off her words. "Plenty of time to turn that around with a few words to your young lawman. During my many years in this world, I've learned there aren't many wrongs that can't be righted, if you sincerely make the effort."

"Even if a soul could lose everything by doing so?" whispered Ivy. Could she do it? Could she essentially risk throwing away every chance for happiness, for herself and Ernest?

"Forgiveness is a powerful word, and most folks find it in their heart after the initial shock wears off." Aunt Minnie clasped her hand. "Sweetheart, there are too many lives at risk if you keep your suspicions to yourself. Too many lives could be ruined from serious injury or even death. You must do the right thing."

"I know, I know. And I'm prepared to do it. Will you come with me, please?" Ivy straightened her back. "I'm not certain I'm strong enough to do this alone."

"Of course, you are. But I will accompany you if you want me to." Aunt Minnie grabbed her hat and reticule and followed Ivy out the schoolhouse door.

The two of them tramped across town to the jailhouse only to discover it dark and totally empty. No drunks even occupied the cells. They closed the door behind them and walked over to the tiny house the two Jones lawmen rented from Mr. Carlyle. That building remained cloaked in darkness, too, and no one answered their knock on the door.

"Where do you suppose Ernest and Donald are?" whispered Ivy, her words sounding loud to her ears in the still of the night.

"I have no idea," replied Aunt Minnie, pulling her shawl tighter around her shoulders. "But we need to scoot on home. Two women out and about alone this time of night is not wise. You can confess all tomorrow morning."

Ivy left Aunt Minnie at the hotel's front doors. Recalling her run-in with that drifter the night her aunt first arrived in town, she needed to heed her aunt's warning and scurry home quickly.

"Are you certain you'll be all right, walking home alone?"

Ivy heard the concern in her aunt's voice. "Of course. I'm only a short distance away. Don't worry and sleep well."

"You too, my angel. I'm so proud of you for deciding to do the right thing." Her aunt hugged her close.

"Thank you. I've been so selfish, thinking only of myself and what's at stake for me. But if someone were to lose his life, I couldn't live with myself."

"Of course, you couldn't. Goodnight. I'll talk to you tomorrow." Aunt Minnie stepped into the hotel and Ivy headed for home.

Ten minutes later, Ivy blew out her breath, relieved to be locked in her living quarters. Home. Safe.

She quickly changed out of her clothes and tugged her cotton nightgown over her head.

"I'll warn Ernest tomorrow," promised Ivy aloud as she climbed into her narrow, squeaky-spring cot. She planned to sneak away at recess time and leave one of the older girls in charge. She would tell Ernest everything. Before it proved too late.

CHAPTER 10

Friday, May 13, 1892

Saddle leather creaked as Blake leaned forward and patted Humbug's neck. Even his mount sensed the excitement and urgency of the situation. Despite having done this dozens of times, Blake's heartbeat raced and his moist hands grasped the reins. There were so many things that could go wrong in the next half hour that he couldn't contemplate all the possibilities. Besides, finding himself dead could be one outcome. Certainly not his first choice. He shivered involuntarily and prayed that the man upstairs would continue watching over his hide.

"Has that banker feller unlocked the door yet?" growled his pa who wasn't known for his patience.

"I ain't seen no sign of him," replied Albert, reining in an excited horse hitched to an old wagon Blake had never seen before. No doubt, he'd stolen the horse and wagon to haul the boxes of payroll funds. His old swaybacked plug wouldn't have been much good at making a getaway. His brother had left him back at the camp.

Blake dug his timepiece out of his waistcoat pocket. "Another five minutes."

Charlie's hand patted the pistol strapped to his leg.

"Itchy fingers, Pa?" Albert grinned like a maniac.

"We agreed there'd be no shooting," blurted Blake, shifting in the saddle and hoping he hadn't sounded overly concerned.

"Dang it, Blake. Just needed to touch my gun for luck. You're worse than a naggin' old woman," complained Charlie.

Blake gritted his teeth, recalling the dozens of times his pa called his mother a naggin' old woman. "Just reminding you that there's no need to invite trouble."

"Long as we surprise 'em, grab the money, and skedaddle a'fore they knows what happened, nobody need git himself shot," reasoned Albert.

Blake knew from experience that their plans needn't veer too far off course before his older brother would be tossing away their original intentions and firing his pistol at someone. He'd never met a man with a shorter fuse, not even his pa. And that was saying something.

"Lookie here!" exclaimed Charlie in a whisper, peering through Blake's monocular spyglass. Fortunately for Blake, his old man hadn't inquired why he would even own such a thing. "He just unlocked the door and poked his head outside for a second," reported his pa, excitement evident in his voice. "Just ducked back inside the bank."

Charlie passed the spyglass back to his youngest offspring, reined his horse around, and leaned forward in the saddle. "Okay, sons, let's go rob us a bank." He grinned from ear to ear, like a child anticipating a new toy, before tugging his bandana into place, hiding the lower portion of his face. He settled his old felt hat lower on his head, partially covering his eyes.

Albert followed suit, seated on the wagon bench.

Blake prayed his counterparts were waiting in their places and this little exercise in law enforcement insanity would go as planned.

Albert glared as his brother. "What ya waitin' fer?"

Blake retracted his spyglass and tucked it back inside his waistcoat pocket. He yanked his bandana into place and settled his Stetson a little lower, concealing his own eyes. "Let's go." *And hope for the best while we're doing it.*

The trio of familial robbers snuck around to the southwest side of town, keeping out of sight, moving around one thicket of bushes after another in hopes of avoiding detection. The wagon wheels rolled along almost soundlessly. Finally, they stood opposite the old weathered wooden building that housed the bank that had been in operation since the town was founded. No one had noticed them approach.

Charlie led the way through the alleyway leading to the front of the bank with Blake following close behind. Albert would drive the wagon up to the front of the bank after they were in place. Blake noticed six horses tethered to a hitching post situated between the building alongside the bank and the bank itself. Did the horseflesh belong to the fellows he hoped they did?

He considered the possibility the manager, Stafford, and the old clerk, Jenkins, and apparently every other fellow who worked in the bank rode horses to work. Or perhaps the mounts belonged to customers patronizing nearby businesses and this hitching post provided a shady spot for the horses to wait. If the robbery turned nasty, Blake prayed no innocent two-footed or four-footed bystanders would be hurt.

"Rush around front, dismount, loop the reins over the post just once and then follow me inside. Three minutes to grab the loot and then we're gone," Charlie reminded his son.

Gritting his teeth, Blake nodded.

Charlie and his mount raced to the front of the bank, his son following.

This was it, thought Blake.

As he and his pa wound their mounts' reins around the hitching post, Albert pulled up with the wagon. He set the brake and leapt to the ground. Five seconds later, the Connors gang rushed up the wooden steps and charged into the Spirit Creek Commerce and Trust Bank, pistols drawn. Instead of immediately hollering orders at those inside as planned, all three of them halted in their tracks.

"What the hell are ya doin' here?" demanded Charlie Connors, glaring at his nemesis and the leader of their rivals, the Bailey gang.

"What are *you* doing here?" growled Walter Bailey.

"We's robbin' the bank, ya idiot," answered Charlie.

"No, you're not. We're robbing the bank." Walter waved his pistol in Charlie's face.

Charlie scoffed, "Ya dang fools couldn't make a proper job of robbin' a cookie jar."

Blake had never encountered a sorrier-looking collection of fellows working on the wrong side of the law. Battered hats covered almost shoulder-length hair, while scruffy beards and moustaches helped disguise their actual appearances. They hadn't even bothered with bandanas. An unpleasant odor permeated the room, diffused into the air from their tattered and soiled clothing. This group of ne'er-do-wells obviously weren't as proficient at robbing banks as were his father and brother. Or else they didn't believe in spending any of the spoils on personal grooming. At least he'd been right about the owners of the horses he'd seen out back.

Blake smiled to himself. His plan had worked perfectly. He even recognized his old buddy, Clayton Ward. They winked at each other when no one was paying them any mind.

"Ha! We bin plannin' this for weeks, Bailey. Step outta my way."

Blake watched as his father bravely, or stupidly depending on a person's point of view, brushed the rival leader's gun barrel aside with his hand.

Walter dropped his arm to his side, the pistol dangling from his fingertips. "Dang it, Connors. We ain't going nowhere. We was here first."

Gregory Stafford, the bank manager, cleared his throat. "Excuse me, gentlemen. If I might make a suggestion."

Both gang leaders spun around and met his eyes, as if they'd forgotten the man was even there.

"What?" they demanded in unison.

Mr. Stafford visibly swallowed hard. "Perhaps you should both just leave, settle this among yourselves, and then one of your gangs might consider returning at another time."

Blake Connors burst into laughter and then coughed to cover his blunder.

Charlie glared at his youngest son and then returned his attention to the bank manager. "Are ya plumb loco, man? We ain't comin' back. Ya'd have the fool sheriff waitin' fer us."

The banker shifted his weight to the other foot. "Well, that wouldn't necessarily be the case. I'd have no idea when you fellows planned to return. The sheriff might be occupied with another matter at the time, and the bank wouldn't be protected at all."

For a moment, it appeared to Blake that Charlie and the other leader were actually considering the feasibility of the suggestion. Blake chuckled to himself, assigned to stand by the front door and watch for a lawman to put in an appearance. If his dang fool father only knew that he'd actually put a lawman in charge of that little task.

Charlie shook his head. "That's the dang stupidest thang I ever heard. We ain't leavin' until we grab that army payroll outta that vault."

"Well, we ain't leaving either," added Walter, stubbornly. He straightened his spine and waved his gun at Charlie. "Besides we were here first and we ain't sharing."

Charlie lifted his pistol a little higher. "Yer a damned idiot if ya think we's leavin' here empty-handed."

"There must be some way that we can divide the funds that will be agreeable to everyone," suggested Gregory, his body vibrating with fear while he displayed unprecedented diplomacy considering the circumstances.

Walter pointed his pistol at Gregory. "Sounds like yer helpin' us with the robbin'. What kind of a dang banker are ya?"

"I'm just endeavoring to keep everyone calm while suggesting a solution that might suit you folks." The manager stepped forward and stuck out a shaky hand. "We haven't been introduced. Gregory Stafford."

Charlie and Walter met eyes.

Charlie shrugged his shoulders. "This is the dang stupidest robbery I ever dun. Git on with it a'fore that damn sheriff shows up."

Blake hadn't peeked out the door lately, having been totally entertained by the charade the robbery had become, and before he realized what was happening, Sheriff Ernest Jones and his brother, Donald, charged through the front door.

"Drop your guns. Now!" demanded Ernest Jones, pointing his pistol at the gang leaders' backs while a couple other fellows followed them in, pistols drawn.

Charlie whipped around and pointed his gun at the young local sheriff.

Sheriff Sanders from Miles City and a couple of his colleagues entered from the back way. "Drop it or I'll shoot," warned Sanders as his deputies moved farther into the room.

"Dammit. This is yer fault, Walter." Charlie set his gun on the floor and raised his hands, all the while glaring at the other leader.

"No it ain't! We were doing fine before you came busting in." Walter reluctantly set his gun down on the plank floor and kicked it toward the sheriff.

Two of the deputies moved forward and started slapping handcuffs on the gang members who'd also set down their weapons and raised their hands.

Suddenly, Blake watched horror struck, as Walter Bailey reached inside his jacket and withdrew a pistol. When he extended his arm and pointed the weapon at Ernest's back a shot rang out. Walter crumpled to the floor.

"Don't nobody else try something stupid," warned Sheriff Sanders, reaching down and checking for a pulse. He shook his head.

"Thanks, Bob," said Ernest, appearing a little shaken.

Soon, every robber was handcuffed and herded out the door, destined for a jail cell, including Blake Connors. Also known among law enforcement folks as undercover Pinkerton agent, Blake Robbins. Fellow agent, Clayton Ward, wore another set of handcuffs and accompanied him out the door.

* * *

Two hours later, Ernest wandered back to the jail cell where he'd locked up Blake. He'd stuck Charlie and Albert in the second cell. No need for Blake to endure their presence if it could be avoided.

He admired Blake more than any man he knew, even Sheriff Sanders. Envied Blake more than he cared to admit also. The man was living Ernest's dream, but now that he'd fallen for Ivy, becoming a Pinkerton agent had lost most of its appeal. Especially when he'd learned all that was involved when working undercover. He could think of a dozen easier ways to make a living.

"Where's Walter Bailey and his bunch?" Blake stood with his back to Ernest, gazing out the cell window at the empty back alley.

"Sheriff Sanders and his deputies escorted the other gang back to Miles City for trial," replied Ernest, slipping the key into the heavy metal lock.

"Did Clayton go with them?"

"Yes, sir. Said to tell you he'd see you later, back in Chicago."

Ernest turned the key and swung the cell door wide open. "I figure the time has come to end this sham."

"Can't say I disagree." Blake strode across the floor and stepped past the young sheriff who slammed the cell door closed again.

Charlie shouted from the other cell, "So, sheriff. Are ya convinced ya made a mistake? Are we gettin' us outta here?"

"No way in hell," muttered Blake, disgust evident in his voice.

"Then why'd the sheriff let you out?" complained Albert, kicking the metal bars of the cell with one booted foot.

"I don't make a habit of locking up my counterparts." Ernest stood hands on hips glaring at the two accused.

Charlie frowned and stared at Blake. "Counterparts?"

"What the hell's a counterpart?" sneered Albert.

"A colleague. An equal," provided Ernest.

Charlie hooted, "You think my son is your equal?"

"No, actually, he's a dang sight better. Has a lot more training. Infinitely more experienced. Probably a better man all around," confessed Ernest. "I don't know as I could do what he does."

Albert sneered at his brother. "Better man? He's an ass. Never willing to take a chance. Always griping about being careful. Wouldn't shoot a frog off a log, never mind anything else."

"That's what makes Blake such a good lawman. Sensible, caring, but serious about his work as well," said Ernest, his words evidence of his admiration.

Blake stood a little taller. "I go by Blake Robbins when I'm working, Pa. Your youngest son has been employed for the past five years as an undercover agent for the Pinkerton Detective Agency headquartered in Chicago. I infiltrated bank-robbing gangs, even a few train-robbing outfits, and I worked with local law enforcement to catch them in the act to ensure they're incarcerated for a good long time."

Charlie's mouth dropped open.

Ernest interjected, "I imagine the Bailey gang will get fifteen years or more for all the jobs that Clayton Ward fellow has witnessed over the years. And you two will be sent to prison for at least that long, maybe longer for everything Blake knows about you."

"Traitor!" shouted Albert.

"I taught you everything I know and this is how you repay me? I hope you rot in Hell, you ungrateful brat," added Charlie. "You'll pay for this."

Blake glanced over at Ernest. "Didn't figure they'd take the news too well."

"Appears, once again you're right."

Blake met his father's eyes. "I told you dozens of times I didn't want the life you lived, but you didn't hear a word I said. Well, I found a way to live my life with dignity and honor and in the way I'd always intended. Doing honest work. Protecting folks from criminals."

Albert slammed his fist against the cell bar. "You're just a damn pansy-ass, good-for-nothing, sonofabitch. Too frightened to take a few chances and do a real man's work."

"Like you do? Hiding behind a gun? Taking what other men have earned through sweat and hard work?" Blake scoffed. "Yeah, that's real manly of you, Albert. I've never seen such a lazy fool in my life, as the likes of you."

Albert thrust his arm out between the metal bars, obviously aiming for Blake's throat, only to discover his reach fell short. "If I ever get out of here, I'll kill you."

"Real brave fellow there," said Ernest, leading Blake to the front room of the jailhouse.

"Yer gonna pay for this!" yelled Albert.

"Nobody crosses me and gets away with it, Blake!" shouted Charlie. "And you're no longer my son."

"More small mercies." Blake poured himself the last few ounces in the bottom of the coffee pot and set it on the small wooden table beside the woodstove. The concoction looked like a fellow could wedge a spoon in it, but it was hot and welcome. He took a sip and acquired an even greater appreciation for Gertie's coffee at the hotel.

"So, Agent Connors, what do we do now?" asked Ernest, draining his own tin cup.

CHAPTER 11

Ernest looked up when the jailhouse door flew open. Businessman and mayor, Randy Barker, strode inside dressed in what other fellows would consider their Sunday best. "Sheriff, what's this wild tale I heard about the Connors gang and Bailey gang both attempting to rob the dang bank at the same time?"

"Not a tale at all." Sheriff Jones pointed his thumb in the direction of the jail cells.

"Evidence is right back there. The other gang was escorted to Miles City by Bob Sanders and his deputies."

"So it *is* true. I was working in the sawmill office when my man returned from a delivery in town. I thought I was hearing things." Barker hung his bowler on a hook by the door and then settled his attention on Blake. "And who might you be?" he inquired.

Ernest waved the mayor toward a chair. "This fellow was one of the bank robbers. Well, not like you'd think."

The mayor frowned. "Ernest, you're making as much sense as a Saturday night drunk reciting a tongue twister."

Blake settled on the other available chair, leaned over, and extended his hand. "Blake Connors, Charlie Connors's youngest son. I'm also a Pinkerton detective working undercover as Blake Robbins."

Deputy Donald Jones charged into the jailhouse, having been sent to purchase coffee at the general store after Ernest used up the last of it brewing his infamous sludge. Spotting Blake casually sipping his coffee, he demanded, "What in blazes is he doing out of his cell?"

Ernest answered, "I let him out. Put on another pot of coffee and I'll explain."

"So you're a Pinkerton!" exclaimed Barker, staring at Blake. The two men shook hands, looking each other over. A broad politician's smile covered the mayor's face.

"Who's a Pinkerton?" demanded Donald, grabbing the coffee pot.

"Him," replied the mayor, indicating Blake.

"The hell he is. He's one of the Connors gang who tried to rob the bank," grumbled Donald, filling the pot from a pail of water on a side table.

"It's true, brother. Blake here is a Pinkerton," insisted Ernest.

Blake leaned back in his chair. "I've always hated what my family did, so I joined the agency several years ago. For the past five years, I've worked undercover infiltrating bank-robbing and train-robbing gangs. Whenever I caught wind of a robbery, I warned local law-enforcement fellows so they could catch the bastards in the act."

Barker scratched his head. "And that's what happened today?"

Ernest understood his boss's confusion. He'd been trying to wrap his own mind around it all, too.

"Yes, sir," replied Blake, beaming with pride. "Two gangs were arrested right here in your town. I knew Bailey's gang planned to steal that payroll. One of our other agents, Clayton Ward, infiltrated their gang a few years back and he warned me about their intentions. So I arranged for my family to rob the same bank at the identical time. All of these criminals are behind bars now."

Barker whistled, shaking his head. "Dang craziest thing I ever heard. A man turning on his family like that."

"Actually, it's not much of a family. Since I turned seventeen, Pa tried to draw me into his life of crime. I couldn't accept what Pa did, forcing my involvement in several robberies when younger. One night, I heard about the Pinkerton Agency from one of Pa's acquaintances who was complaining bitterly about being arrested by one of their agents a few years back. I figured there'd be no better way to rid myself of that life than to go after folks like my pa and brother."

"And you've done this for several years?"

"I've helped capture my share of outlaws."

Donald Jones leaned against his brother's desk, arms folded across his chest while the coffee brewed. "But today your own family was arrested."

"Awhile back, I'd finally had enough of the deceptions, and I put in a special request to my superiors. They agreed that my family could be arrested with this last robbery. And just a week ago I heard grumblings from a couple of Pa's cronies that a Pinkerton agent would be getting his comeuppance. I wasn't certain if it was me or someone else they'd discovered, but I suspected after all these years eventually my cover would be shot to hell. Headquarters agreed I shouldn't work undercover any longer." Blake sighed. "I'll be assigned to a different area of work now."

Ernest cleared his throat. "Actually, Mayor, I was sworn to secrecy, but agent Connors shared his true identity with me, spilled the beans about the upcoming robbery, and confided his part in the intended capture of those responsible."

"You knew!" exclaimed Barker.

"Yes sir, I did. But I couldn't say anything. Frankly, after I talked to Blake I felt plumb out of my league. I travelled to Miles City since he'd warned me that another agent had been in contact with Sheriff Bob Sanders concerning the same matter."

"I'd heard you travelled to Miles City a few days ago," said the mayor.

"Sheriff Sanders and I worked out a plan. Bob and his deputies showed up at the bank at the same time as Donald and me and a couple of fellows I deputized just in case. We didn't want anyone escaping. And the other agent arrived in town with the Bailey gang." Ernest grimaced. "Worked out just dandy except Walter Bailey pulled a gun, aimed it at my back, and Sanders had to kill him."

The mayor frowned and scratched his head for a few moments. "So, nobody actually robbed the bank."

"Couldn't have." Ernest chuckled. "Those boxes that arrived the other day were just a decoy, filled with old newspapers. The real payroll is safely stashed in a bank in Miles City, ready for the army to hand it out to their soldiers."

"Dammit to hell, Ernest," blurted Donald, glaring daggers at this brother. He straightened up and wagged his finger at him. "Do you know I've hardly slept a wink in two nights, worrying about that blasted payroll? Considering the possibility somebody might rob the bank because of it? You couldn't see fit to let me in on this?"

"Don't you think I would have if I was allowed? I've only slept a few hours, too. Worrying about what all could go wrong when those bastards actually tried to hold up the bank."

Donald waved off his brother's comments. Cursing under his breath, he poured fresh-brewed coffee for everyone, grabbing a fairly clean, tin cup off a wooden shelf above the table for the mayor.

Ernest met Blake's eyes. "I've got a confession to make. When you first showed up in town and told me who you were, I was as jealous as a jilted lover. Then as time wore on and all the things that could go wrong started running through my mind, I've got to tell you something. Dang if I don't admire you even more, but I don't know if I could handle what you do every day, all year long. It might send me around the bend."

Blake slapped Ernest on the back. "It's stressful work. Always looking over your shoulder. Always suspicious of everyone around you. Constantly watching everything that's going on. I guess not every man is cut out for this type of work."

"Well, I'm quite content to remain a small town sheriff. I won't be bitching about having to arrest a bunch of rowdy cowhands on Saturday nights ever again," admitted Ernest. "Give me a quiet life with a good woman and a bunch of kids and I'll be happy for the rest of my days."

"I hear you," agreed the mayor, who was a happily-married father of five with another on the way.

"Well, Ernest, I'm delighted you're going to be settling down with Ivy Patterson."

Ernest reared back and met Blake's eyes. "So, you didn't set your sights on her, too?"

"Nope." Blake smiled. "Ivy Patterson is my little sister."

* * *

Ernest mulled over this information for a few seconds; he nearly couldn't believe what he heard. "Then that means those two varmints cooling their heels back in that jail cell are her father and her brother?"

"Yes, they are," confirmed Blake.

"And you didn't feel it necessary to admit you knew Ivy until now?" growled Ernest.

Blake stood, staring at him. "Well, I didn't consider it really mattered."

Ernest leapt to his feet and slammed his mug on the desk. Coffee sloshed over the side and puddled on his desk, soaking several sheets of paper. "When Ivy first arrived in Spirit Creek, she told everyone she was an orphan. Didn't have a soul in the world. No family and only a few friends she'd met at normal school. Fabricated a tale about an orphanage."

Blake stood, silent.

Mayor Barker sat in his chair, mouth agape.

"I guess her story was all a bunch of bull dung," said Donald.

Blake glanced at the deputy and then turned back to Ernest. "Well, it weren't the truth. But I suppose she didn't want folks judging her based on who her kin were. I know I didn't. Hated admitting to people that I was Charlie Connors's son, even when working undercover. I imagine it would be even worse for a woman, especially someone who'd worked hard all her life to become someone she could be proud of, like Ivy has."

Ernest shook his head. "No matter how you try to pretty it up, she told us lies. Plain and simple. Every person in this town. Lied right to their face."

"Ivy ran away from home shortly after our ma passed away."

"Just because she turned her back on her kin, don't mean her family just disappears from this world," reasoned Donald.

"He's just defending *his sister*." Ernest nearly choked on the words. Some lawman he'd proven himself to be. He couldn't believe how badly he'd been taken in by the woman he loved. Now, he wasn't certain he did love her. Hearing the truth, he'd suddenly realized the extent of her deception.

"Damn right, I'm defending her. You claim to love her, proposed marriage. And here you stand condemning her."

Ernest turned on Blake. "I can't condone liars."

"Ivy is so much more than a girl who told a couple lies. She took our mother's maiden name as her new surname, hated the name Connors and all that it represented. Ma's sister, our aunt, raised her. Ivy excelled at school, attended normal school, graduated top of her class."

"I recognize an intelligent woman when I meet one. But it appears she's worked as industriously at her lying as she has at everything else." Ernest opened the jailhouse door, tossed the dregs from the bottom of his coffee cup, and slammed the door closed again.

Mayor Barker stood and approached the sheriff. "Now, Ernest, I reckon this news comes as a shock, but you've got to admit one thing. Miss Ivy is one of the best teachers this town has ever hired. She's church-going, always behaves like a lady. Hell, she has put in more hours doing volunteer work for this community than either of us could count."

Blake set his coffee mug on the corner of the sheriff's desk. "Ivy is making an honest living as a schoolteacher. The mayor just admitted she's a valued member of this community. You're lucky to have a woman like that in your life, Jones."

"Still don't change the fact she lied to the entire town," insisted Ernest. His strong sense of right and wrong wouldn't allow him to even consider moving past what she'd done. Besides, years ago, a girl had lied to him, made promises she didn't keep. Just up and left town with her family, promised to write and keep in touch. He'd never heard from her again. He'd thought better of Ivy. Apparently, he'd been wrong.

Donald chimed in, "She might have told a fib or two, big brother, but that girl truly loves your sorry behind. Nearly had a conniption fit when I told her you were off in Miles City. Seemed plumb near worried to death about you."

Ernest couldn't fathom the extent of the lies Ivy had told him. Were there more things she lied about besides who her family was? Could he ever trust her again? He somehow doubted it. From the time he could walk, he'd been taught right from wrong. And lying was just plain wrong. No exceptions to the rule.

All right, maybe he could understand her telling the community she had no ties to a family. Divulged no ties to her past. But they were engaged! She should have trusted him enough, loved him enough to confess the truth to the man she intended to marry and spend the rest of her life with. But no. She hadn't. Just proved she didn't love him enough. His chest hurt from that realization, even more than the feeling of betrayal he experienced upon hearing about the deception she'd lived by for all these years.

He grabbed his Stetson off the hook by the door, fixing to make his escape before he started tearing up. Sheriffs didn't cry, even broken-hearted ones. "I need to tell Ivy our plans have changed. I can't abide a liar, and I sure as hell ain't marrying one. The engagement is off."

* * *

All morning, Ivy had more trouble concentrating than her youngest, attention-challenged student. Finally, recess time arrived. The children seemed to take longer than usual to assemble outside for play time. Ivy assigned one of the older Jones girls and a future sister-in-law to supervise everyone, promising to return in a few minutes.

Ivy unclipped her watch and handed it over to the fourteen-year-old. "If I haven't returned by quarter to the hour, take the children inside. The older ones can read. Could you please help the younger ones with their printing?"

"Yes, Miss Patterson," confirmed the student.

Ivy strode out of the schoolyard at a very unladylike pace, arms pumping in her haste, headed for the jailhouse. Time was of the essence. She needed to talk to Ernest and then rush back to resume her teaching duties.

"My goodness, Ivy Patterson, where are you off to in such a hurry?" exclaimed June Davidson, stepping aside on the wooden sidewalk outside the hotel to prevent a collision.

"I need to speak with Ernest," she explained as she passed.

"Give him my best," called June, returning to sweeping the sidewalk. "I hope everything is all right, all things considered."

Ivy halted in her tracks and turned. "Why wouldn't everything be all right?"

"Well, with the attempted bank robbery and all…"

Ivy didn't wait to hear the rest of Mrs. Davidson's explanation. She hoisted her skirts and ran for the jailhouse. Tears burned the back of her eyes with the realization that she'd waited too long. She was too late to warn Ernest. Too late to prevent the robbery.

Her breakfast threatened to make a reappearance. She swallowed hard. Had Ernest been hurt? Had anyone been shot? Mrs. Davidson hadn't indicated there'd been any shooting, but Ivy hadn't waited long enough to hear the entire story. Perhaps the robbers got away before they were confronted by the lawmen. But Mrs. Davidson had said 'attempted' bank robbery.

If anyone had gotten hurt she would just die!

Ivy charged into the jailhouse and immediately spotted Ernest standing just inside the doorway with his back to her.

"I need to tell Ivy our plans have changed. I can't abide a liar, and I sure as hell ain't marrying one. The engagement is off."

Ivy gasped aloud and Ernest whipped around.

"What do you mean, the engagement is off?" Ivy's knees buckled and she would have landed on the floor if someone hadn't grabbed her around the waist. She looked up and met Blake's eyes.

"Are you all right?" Her brother gripped her tightly, concern evident in his voice.

How could anyone believe her to be unaffected by what Ernest said? "June Davidson told me about an attempted bank robbery. Why aren't you in a jail cell?" She glared at her brother.

Blake chuckled. "I was."

Ivy gasped. "You escaped?"

"Ernest let me out."

"I…I…I don't understand," she stammered.

"For someone without any kin, Ivy, your family members are filling up my jail cells rapidly," accused Ernest.

"You know?" gasped Ivy, staring at Ernest. She grimaced seeing the pain of her betrayal in his eyes.

He pointed a finger at Blake. "Seems one of them is actually a Pinkerton detective working undercover."

"A what?" Ivy met Blake's eyes.

"It's true."

"About your family? Your lies? I know all of it. And we're done." Ernest turned to leave.

"You can't mean it. I love you so much." Ivy struggled out of Blake's hold, grabbed Ernest's arm, preventing him from stepping out the door. "Despite my fears that you'd turn your back on me if you ever learned the truth, I came to tell you everything the other night anyway. You weren't here. Donald told me you were in Miles City."

"Convenient for you," muttered Ernest.

"Unfortunate. I'd decided I'd risk everything including your love and our future together to warn you that my father and brothers would probably rob the bank in a few days. I wanted to keep you and everyone else in the community safe. But you were never here. I tried so hard to find you, tell you it all. I prayed our love was strong enough, that you would realize why I did it and understand."

"Guess you were wrong."

"About not telling you who I was?"

"Wrong about how strongly we loved each other," he clarified.

Ivy's heart almost broke as she slipped the beautiful ruby ring off her finger and handed it to him.

Ernest stuffed it into his denim trouser pocket and folded his arms across his chest.

Ivy gazed at the other men in the room through a veil of unshed tears. "What have I done?" Her tears flowed unchecked. Sobbing uncontrollably, she raced out the door.

CHAPTER 12

Ernest stared at the empty doorway, feeling like he'd been kicked hard in the gut by one of Luke Carlyle's steers. His entire world had just walked through it. Had he over-reacted to this whole business with Ivy and her family?

Hell, no.

And the proof occupied one of his cells. Ivy should have told him the truth. End of debate. Admittedly though, he wouldn't have been caught off guard by the bank robbery since he'd been apprised of the entire thing weeks ago. But she had no way of knowing that.

What if he hadn't known? What if he'd walked into the robbery in progress unprepared? What if someone in town, an innocent citizen, had done so and been killed? A pregnant woman like Sadie Maxwell? Or a defenseless matron like Elizabeth Waverly? Or a man of the cloth like Reverend Gerald? The list could go on forever.

"You're a damn fool," declared Donald.

Ernest startled, his brother's accusation drawing him out of his musings.

"Maybe so, but I won't marry a liar."

"Aren't you ever going to get past that?" blurted Donald, annoyance evident in his voice. "So she didn't tell you who her family was? Not everyone is as fortunate as you and me, brother. Few people are born into a family like the Jones clan."

"Hear, hear," agreed the mayor. "Lots of folks would give their eye teeth to have been raised by someone like Florence Jones. Your ma is a saint. Patient. Understanding. Moral. And an excellent cook to boot. Hell, we haven't enjoyed a decent meal in weeks. She can adopt *me* if she wants."

"Is your wife still under the weather?" asked Ernest, welcoming the change of topic. He hated the fact his private business had been under discussion yet again.

"This pregnancy is the most difficult one she's ever endured." Mayor Barker smiled. "I'm hoping this is an indication she's carrying a boy this time. What do I need with daughter number six?"

"Six!" exclaimed Blake. "You could almost field one of those baseball teams I've read about by yourself. Nine on a team, I believe."

The mayor scowled. "My daughters are young ladies. They won't be playing any manly games like baseball, thank you very much."

"Just teasing." Blake held up his hands in surrender.

"Keep your comments to yourself." The mayor turned his attention back to his sheriff. "Now, Ernest, you'd best think on this for a day or two before you decide it's all over for certain between you and Miss Ivy."

Donald chimed in, "I'd be surprised if that ring don't start burning a hole in your pocket. I'd wager it just might find its way back onto that lovely girl's finger."

"I doubt that very much…" began Ernest.

The mayor held up his hand. "Just give it a little time. Don't throw away a good thing over a little hurt pride. So she didn't tell us the truth. I can understand completely why she did it."

Ernest stood hands on hips. "And why would that be?" he demanded.

"Do you suppose for a minute Ronald Waverly would have hired her had she included in her employment letter *'the bank robber, Charlie Connors, is my father'?* Her employment inquiry would have landed in the trash bin faster than you could sneeze. And the town would have missed out on one of the best teachers we've ever employed."

Ernest's hands dropped to his sides. In his head, he knew the mayor had a point and was right. But he loved Ivy so much that he was incapable of wrapping his mind around how badly she deceived him. He hadn't suspected a thing. Some Pinkerton detective he would have made.

* * *

Ivy had dried her tears when she returned to the schoolhouse, standing outside the classroom before entering. Holding in her emotions after losing Ernest's love and respect had nearly killed her, but she couldn't let her students down.

Only one of the older girls had noticed she no longer wore her ring when she returned, but after a purposeful glare in her direction, the student hadn't voiced the question evident on her face.

Ivy completed the day's work and sent the children home. Finally, she dragged her aching body and broken heart into her room in back and burst into tears. It was over. The suspected robbery. The endless secrets. Her hopes and dreams of a life with Ernest. Everything. How could she go on?

Ernest Jones meant the world to her. She'd never find another man whom she could love as much as she loved him. But she'd hurt him so badly—she'd witnessed just how deeply she'd wounded him in his eyes earlier at the jailhouse—that there was no hope of winning his forgiveness. No chance at all. And rightly so. She deserved to lose him for what she'd done.

It seemed like hours later before the sobbing subsided. Deciding she had the rest of her life to mourn the loss of her one true love, Ivy forced herself to straighten up and face reality. Ernest no longer wanted her, and folks would certainly notice the absence of the ring, including her aunt.

Her aunt!

How could Ivy have forgotten Aunt Minnie? Since her arrival in town, her aunt expected Ivy to join her for supper in the hotel's dining room every night. She was probably seated there now, patiently waiting for her niece.

Ivy leapt to her feet, grabbed her shawl, and dashed out the door.

As she strode down the sidewalk, headed for the hotel, Ivy ran all the day's events over in her mind. For a brief moment, she considered what might happen if the school committee learned she'd left the children in the care of one of her students. She'd done it before, if one of the children had been hurt and she'd needed to escort them to Doc's office. But today's decision to do so had been solely for person reasons.

Ivy tripped over a loose board and she gasped aloud. "What if Mr.

Waverly fires me for lying about my name? For claiming I hadn't a family?"

Tears filled her eyes again with this new possibility. She'd already lost Ernest, but if she lost the job she loved as well, she couldn't go on. But she deserved it. She should have had more faith in Ernest and their love for each other. And she certainly shouldn't have lied to her employer.

In hindsight, Ivy decided Ernest had been absolutely justified in sending her packing. Had their situations been reversed, she never would have wanted to see him again. Probably. Maybe. She still loved him so much.

Ivy continued toward the hotel as she pondered her situation. She'd come so close to having it all. Happiness. A forever love. A husband and children. Everything she'd ever wanted.

Now, all of it was gone. And she had no one to blame but herself.

CHAPTER 13

"I'll go check on Ivy," offered Blake. "She was pretty upset."

Mayor Barker and Donald nodded, but Ernest just slumped into his chair behind the desk. Blake headed toward the door but halted in his tracks when the open doorway filled with a man's mammoth form.

"Hello, I'm Samuel Burton."

Blake shook hands with him. "Blake Connors."

"Connors." The man stuck a familiar badge in Blake's face.

"You're a Pinkerton agent?" The question sounded a little harsh even to Blake's ears, but the fellow acted rather brusque. Maybe he resented being assigned to a small community like Spirit Creek, preferred working in a large city. "I wasn't aware you were headed our way."

"Worked a case in Butte, but headquarters sent me a telegram with orders to head over here when the job was completed." Burton glanced at the other men in the room.

"Sorry, Burton. Mayor Randy Barker is over there by the window, and the fellow seated at the desk is Sheriff Ernest Jones. That's his brother, Deputy Donald Jones."

"Pleased to meet you folks," said Burton.

The other men extended their own acknowledgments of the introductions, followed by handshakes all around.

"I hear you had a bit of excitement here today." Burton removed his hat and twirled it in his hand.

"Captured the Bailey and the Connors gangs. Attempted to rob the bank. Both are locked away; Baileys in Miles City, Connors are here. I'd call it a productive day's work," commented Ernest, leaning back in his chair and crossing his arms over his chest.

"Unfortunately, Walter Bailey was killed, but he pulled a gun on Ernest here," justified the mayor.

"Congratulations, gentlemen," said Burton. "Why the glum expressions then? Can't be over Bailey?"

"It's a private matter," blurted Donald. "Nothing to do with the actual incident itself."

Blake glanced at Donald and nodded. He appreciated the man's quick response, assuring the personal matter remained among the locals.

Burton's gaze scanned the room. When no further explanation was forthcoming, he frowned. "All right, well then, I'll head over to the hotel and register for a room. I'll hang around town for another day or so until I receive additional instructions from headquarters."

"Appreciate it," said Ernest. "Don't imagine there'll be any trouble. Just waiting to hear about the trials. The Baileys were escorted to Miles City by the town's local lawmen who helped with the arrest. We'll keep the Connors here."

"Gentlemen." Burton headed out the door.

Blake watched from the doorway as he untied a spirited pure-black horse from the hitching post and mounted up. Burton waved as he headed for the hotel.

"What do you make of him?" asked the mayor, when Blake stepped back inside.

"I don't know. Looks vaguely familiar," he admitted. "Perhaps we worked a case together once years ago. Seems odd I didn't receive notification of his pending arrival. Mind you, I've been up to my ears in bank robbers for weeks now, so my boss might have assumed I'd just appreciate the help if it proved necessary. Or perhaps no one at headquarters wanted to risk tipping off our plans to anyone."

"I suppose." Ernest straightened in his chair. "Seems odd though. Showing up after all the excitement's over. You would think they would have timed his arrival better."

"Perhaps your fellows at headquarters just figured you would appreciate help transporting those men for trial." Mayor Barker moved toward the door. "Well, I'm heading home to check on the missus. Then I'm gathering up my daughters and taking them to the hotel for supper. Just because an expectant wife isn't feeling up to eating don't mean the rest of us should starve."

The others offered their agreement.

"Thanks for coming by, Mayor," Ernest leapt to his feet and shook the man's hand.

"Think nothing of it. I'm just happy to see your plans played out so well."

"Good day, Mayor Barker," called Donald, as the man slipped out the door.

Blake stood hands on hips. "I wonder if my sister has calmed down yet. Perhaps Aunt Minnie has quieted her some by now."

"Aunt Minnie? That lady who arrived a few days ago is her aunt?" exclaimed Ernest.

"Yes, she's our mother's spinster sister who raised Ivy. They're quite close. I understand more like mother and daughter." Blake chuckled. "Perhaps they're plotting your comeuppance for breaking my sister's heart."

Donald burst into laughter. "Would serve him right. Ivy's a wonderful young lady. Might consider courting her myself if…"

"*Don't* even think about it." Ernest stared daggers at his younger brother.

Blake slapped Donald on the back. "Now that I think about it, you'd make a fine brother-in-law."

"Thank you, Blake. I'd consider it an honor to…"

Ernest rounded the desk with fire in his eyes.

Donald grabbed his hat off the hook by the door. "Gotta go, Blake. Rounds to make."

"I'll give you a hand."

Both men raced out the door and down the stairs. Each man untied his mount's reins in record time and leapt onto his horse. Blake glanced behind him. Ernest stood scowling in the doorway, watching them ride north in the direction of the local saloons.

* * *

Ivy hurried through the streets of Spirit Creek, offering only a quick wave to everyone who called out a greeting to her, intent on reaching Aunt Minnie as soon as possible. The two of them met at six o'clock sharp for supper together every evening. Ivy checked her timepiece and grimaced. Six twenty.

How would she explain her tardiness?

Ivy slowed her pace as she walked through the busy hotel lobby, waved to June Davidson standing behind the registration desk, and continued on into the dining room. At least two dozen patrons conversed over their meals and high-spirited laughter accompanied many conversations. The merriment only magnified the contrast to Ivy's blue mood. The sounds of dishes rattling and verbal exchanges between the kitchen workers and customers as the staff moved among the various tables added to the noise level in the dining room. Ivy's temples throbbed with the beginnings of a headache.

Minnie Patterson sat at their usual table, dressed to the nines as usual, looking completely out of place in a small town like Spirit Creek. Her aunt dabbed at her eyes with a lacy white handkerchief, sniffled softly, and muttered to herself. No doubt, her troubled expression was caused by something more serious than waiting for a tardy dinner companion.

"I'm so sorry. I completely lost track of time," offered Ivy as an apology.

Her aunt didn't acknowledge her presence.

"Is something wrong, Auntie?" Ivy reached out and touch the wrinkled hand resting on the blue satin dress.

Her aunt startled. "Oh, Ivy, I didn't notice that you'd arrived."

"What's wrong?" Ivy suspected her aunt had heard about the attempted robbery. The entire town would know about it by now.

"They did it. Just like you suspected they would." Aunt Minnie met her eyes. "I see you've heard the news also. Your eyes are all red and puffy from crying."

Ivy nodded, hiding her left hand in the tablecloth's folds.

"Last I heard, the bank robbers were caught in the act. Did you talk to Ernest? Are Charlie, Blake and Albert in jail?" Her aunt leaned forward in her seat.

"They were."

"Were? My goodness, did they escape?"

"Heavens no, Auntie. I can't see that happening."

"Then what do you mean?"

Ivy sighed. "I hardly know where to begin."

"Well, start talking, I've already lost my appetite." Aunt Minnie placed her arms on the table. "Tell me everything."

Ivy related what she'd learned at the jailhouse, and Aunt Minnie gasped with every new detail.

"An undercover Pinkerton detective!" exclaimed her aunt. "I must say, I'm quite impressed. At least, Blake's working on the right side of the law."

"I'm very proud of him." Ivy smiled for the first time today. "One bit of good news resulting from all this."

"I imagine Charlie and Albert don't consider it good news."

"I don't suppose so, but there's nothing they can do about it. They broke the law, they will pay the price." Ivy tapped the tablecloth with her index finger for emphasis.

"So, why all the tears? Surely, you don't feel sorry for them being caught?" A horrified expression accompanied the question.

"Goodness, no. Father and Albert deserve every year in jail they serve." Ivy glanced away, her eyes filling with tears. "Something else happened when…"

"Lord in heaven!" exclaimed Aunt Minnie. "Please don't tell me Ernest was…"

Ivy gasped and whipped around. "No! Oh, had he been killed I would never have survived it."

"Then what has you so glum?"

Ivy produced her left hand for her aunt's inspection. "When Ernest learned that Blake was my brother, he realized I'd lied about having a family. That I lied about being the daughter of a gang of bank robbers."

Her aunt's hand flew to her mouth.

"Ernest called off the engagement so I returned his ring. It's over. Except for you and Blake and my teaching job, I've lost everything that matters to me." Ivy burst into tears.

"Oh, my precious girl!" Aunt Minnie leapt out of her chair and pulled Ivy into a tight embrace. "Everything will work out. Just give that young man of yours a few days to come to terms with what you did. He'll realize you meant no harm, that you were ashamed of your parentage."

Ivy shook her head. "I don't think so."

"Ernest comes from good people, and folks like that don't hold grudges," reasoned her aunt.

"Honest, upstanding citizens like the Jones family don't condone liars either. My foolish lies have sealed my fate." Ivy wiped her tear-stained cheeks with her handkerchief. "I just pray I don't lose my teaching position as well."

* * *

The Pinkerton detective slumped in an oversized wicker chair on The Spirit Creek Hotel's veranda, some distance from the front door. He gazed into the distance, legs extended out in front of him, ankles crossed, tanned hands stacked one atop the other on his belly.

Ernest guessed he'd sought out a private spot for a few moment's reflection. When word got out there was a Pinkerton in town, all the townsfolk who'd encountered the poor man had plied him with questions about the robbery and the notorious outlaws and the agent himself. "Are you contemplating life?"

Blake's head whipped up, his startled expression proving the other fellow's suggestion viable. He straightened in the chair. "Just running the day's activities over in my head, wondering if we could have done anything differently."

"Why would you harbor doubts?" Ernest settled into a matching chair beside him. "I figured everything went like clockwork. Those fellows couldn't have been more shocked when Donald, Bob and I, and all of our men, charged in there. Too bad Arthur MacDonald's camera wasn't set up. What I wouldn't give to have a photograph of that."

Blake chuckled. "I'd have paid good money to record the expressions on their faces."

Ernest lit a cigar and blew a smoke ring. "Wouldn't have worked though."

"Why do you say that?" Blake waved away the offer of one. "No thanks."

"Well, we can't have an undercover Pinkerton detective in a photograph, would end your undercover career right quick," explained Ernest.

Blake laughed. "Oh, it's ended all right. When headquarters gave the go ahead to have my family arrested, I knew my work was destined for history. Word will get around about who Charlie Connors' youngest son really was. As of today, Blake Robbins is dead and laid to rest, I'm afraid."

"I heard your father and brother threatening revenge. I guess you're a mite worried that they'll make good on it, if they ever get released from prison. Might be several years from now, but still."

"Ernest, I've been living on borrowed time for years. Ever since I first went undercover. I've infiltrated more gangs, put more fellows in prison, than I care to count. It became only a matter of time before it all wound down and I returned to more sedate cases. But I can't say I won't be looking over my shoulder every minute. No telling when the past will sneak up on a fellow."

Ernest watched the range of emotions crossing Blake's face as he spoke. Pride in a job well done. Uncertainty about his future. Worry about himself and probably his sister and aunt, too. "Hell of a way to live. You ever consider just ending it with the Pinkerton agency? Return to society as a regular lawman? Maybe hire on in some town as sheriff?" For a moment, Ernest considered himself perhaps lucky to have just remained in Spirit Creek and not pursued more lofty goals in life. He hadn't considered this down side to the whole business of being a Pinkerton.

"About a dozen times a day, most weeks. Especially when I'm knee deep in criminals and waiting to get hit by a bullet at any moment." Blake grimaced.

"Bob Sanders is a retired Texas Ranger. Married a local gal from Miles City and now he works there as a sheriff. Seems happily married and dang content with his new lot in life," suggested Ernest. "You might be bored to tears though with nothing more than breaking up bar brawls, but at least you'd be alive."

"Don't think I haven't given retirement serious consideration." Blake peeked over at Ernest and met his eyes. "Even more so since I arrived here."

"I heard you were quite taken with Gertie," whispered Ernest, his thumb pointing behind him. They were seated outside the row of dining room windows. "Her twin sister married a local rancher a while back."

"She has a twin?" blurted Blake.

"Yep, spitting image." Ernest chuckled. "I heard Gracie's with child, so don't worry that they might play a joke on you and you wouldn't be able to tell them apart. Besides I imagine Cody Maxwell might have a few choice words for you if he caught you kissing his wife."

Blake glared at him. "Lot of help you'd be. I wouldn't put it past you to mix them up on purpose to see how I did."

"Evening, gentlemen," boomed Samuel Burton's voice, the volume magnified in the quiet night air as he strode up the hotel steps and crossed the veranda's plank floor.

Blake and Ernest nodded a greeting, and Blake pointed to a small wooden chair across from them.

Burton waved off the suggestion, leaned against the veranda railing with one booted foot crossed over the other. "What were the two of you discussing so intently?

"Retirement," stated Blake, before Ernest could answer otherwise.

A frown crossed Burton's face.

"You ever consider retiring, Samuel?" asked Ernest.

"Well…well, now…I can't say…" blustered the Pinkerton.

"You can't tell me you haven't seriously considered retiring when you were up to your ears in trouble of some kind," suggested Blake.

Samuel straightened, stood feet slightly apart, appearing totally stunned by the question. "Well, I suppose I haven't found myself in as many life and death situations as you. Haven't been double-crossing any of my former acquaintances, friends, even family. Been just working regular cases."

"Well, I've thought about it more times than I care to consider."

Samuel nodded at Blake and mumbled, "I suppose if you wanted to retire it could be arranged."

Ernest piped up, "Would be the Pinkerton's loss. Blake's an excellent detective."

"Well, I'm turning in for the night. Be heading back to Chicago tomorrow or the next day."

Blake's head whipped up. "Did you receive a telegraph from headquarters, Burton?"

"Not yet. But I expect I'll hear soon enough. Not much sense in me hanging around here. You fellows have everything under control." Samuel touched his hat brim and headed toward the hotel's front doors. "Goodnight, gentlemen."

"Goodnight," said Blake.

Ernest met his counterpart's eyes and added absently, "Goodnight, Burton."

The remaining two men remained seated, lost in their own thoughts for a few minutes. Shopkeepers Ronald and Elizabeth Waverly, partaking of an evening stroll, passed by on the wooden boardwalk and appeared lost in their own conversation. Chirping crickets and an owl's hoot from a nearby tree were the only other sounds that pierced the silence.

Blake tipped his head to one side. "I just can't put my finger on it."

"What?"

"Burton's tone of voice sounded a little, I don't know, disapproving? Is that the word I'm looking for?" Blake shook his head. "His reaction to the question of retirement seemed a little odd. Don't most fellows look forward to the day when they can retire, especially if the work is stressful or perhaps no longer fulfilling?"

"I reckon they do. Pa's complained to Ma so many times about looking forward to the day when he can just bounce grandchildren on his knee that I've lost count," confided Ernest.

Blake leaned forward, forearms resting on knees. "Pa, too. Wanted to make that one big haul. Spend his time with his feet up and a drink in his hand all day and some woman in his bed every night."

"Now that you mention it, Burton sounded shocked that you'd be discontent enough to retire. Like he expected you were having the time of your life putting criminals behind bars. As if that's all you lived for," added Ernest.

"Maybe he just loves his work more than most men." Blake leaned back in his chair. "One of those fellows who can't fathom doing anything else. No desire to settle down with a wife and family."

"I guess some men think like that. Loners they call them."

Blake glanced over at Ernest. "I've met a few. Eyes as dark as coal. Almost without a soul. Know what I mean?"

Ernest shivered. "Jimmy George Barkley. Fellow who lived here for a spell a few years back."

Blake wagged a finger in Ernest's direction. "Pa mentioned him to me. Something about getting himself killed around these parts."

"No loss." Ernest paled. "That sounded a little cold-hearted. But the fellow abused his wife and didn't care a hoot for his own son. Robbed banks and trains, most useless excuse for a man I've ever met."

"Whoa! Glad I didn't have to tangle with him." Blake stood.

Ernest leap to his feet. "Don't worry about Burton's opinion of you."

"I think he considers me a quitter. Or someone who doesn't take the work seriously enough."

"Bull dung. If you consider retiring, it's your decision and nobody else's."

"Thanks, Ernest. I appreciate that." Blake settled his arm around the other lawman's shoulders. "So, are you and Ivy truly over, or are you reconsidering proposing again?"

"I don't know, Blake. I find it nearly impossible to trust someone again, once they lie or cheat. I've still got some thinking to do. Just dropped by to see if I could catch a glimpse of Ivy. Make sure she was doing all right. I hadn't heard any mention that she'd needed to see Doc or anything, so I guess she's not that troubled."

"I imagine she's hurting. She loves you. No doubt about that. But I'm staying out of it. Whatever is decided is between the two of you and no one else." Blake slapped Ernest's back and turned to leave. He stopped and glanced over his shoulder. "In my opinion though, you'd make a fine brother-in-law."

"Thanks," whispered Ernest. "You would, too."

CHAPTER 14

Saturday, May 14, 1892

Ernest wandered into the Spirit Creek Hotel for an early lunch, accompanied by Blake Connors and Samuel Burton. Chairs scraped the wooden floor as they seated themselves at a round wooden table. Sunshine streamed in through the open window and a light spring breeze ruffled the floral-patterned curtains.

Gertie patted her hair and then dashed over to take their orders.

Ernest caught Blake admiring how well the pretty blue dress fit the waitress's curves in all the right places. Her hair shone, tied back with a matching ribbon, and her lips were reddened by some means. Had she anticipated Blake's patronage this morning? Ernest hoped whenever he encountered Ivy in public, he hadn't looked like a lovesick calf, the way his buddy, Blake, did right now.

"What can I get you?" Gertie blushed, gazing at Blake and ignoring the others.

Ernest cleared his throat. "What is the special?"

"Just chicken stew and biscuits. No pie or pudding or nothing. Cook says she thinks she's coming down with something." Gertie leaned in closer and whispered near Blake's ear. "Don't tell Mrs. Davidson I said this, but Cook went looking for her errant husband a couple of nights ago. Caught him with a saloon girl seated on his lap at the Joker's Wild. Her gizzard has been in a twitch over that for days now. And Cook won't allow just anyone into her kitchen ever since you-know-who set the place on fire.

That woman has been simply impossible to work with."

Samuel's mouth dropped open. "Someone set the hotel's kitchen on fire?"

"Quite a while ago now. Nearly burned down the whole damn place. Thank goodness the water brigade got the fire out before too much damage was done." Ernest shared that little tidbit of town history with the visitor.

"We'll all have the day's special." Blake placed their orders, looking pointedly at Ernest, he added, "And please bring some coffee. Best I've tasted in ages."

Gertie's face flamed. "Thank you. I usually make it myself," she gushed and stared into Blake's eyes.

Ernest guffawed. "Today please, Gertie."

The waitress glared at the sheriff and then scurried toward the kitchen. She returned a minute later with three cups of coffee atop a small metal tray. "I hope you like it." She looked directly at Blake and then headed off to another table to take more orders.

"Am I missing something here?" Samuel frowned.

"Prime suspect in the reasoning behind Blake contemplating retirement," teased Ernest.

Samuel bobbed his head and chuckled. "If you need assistance in questioning the suspect, let me know. Always happy to offer my opinion."

"Aren't the two of you just the funniest fellows," grumbled Blake.

The food arrived, delivered to the table by the scowling middle-aged cook herself, dressed in a brown calico dress covered by an enormous white apron.

"Thank you, ma'am," offered Samuel.

She mumbled something and then the sour-faced woman returned to the kitchen.

The men tucked into their meals.

Blake swallowed his first mouthful. "Tasty."

"I agree. As long as she didn't add a little arsenic," mumbled Samuel, his mouth full.

Ernest waved his fork at Blake to get his attention, and then swallowed before speaking. "I forgot to mention I received a telegraph from Bob Sanders this morning. The Bailey gang members are snug as bugs in their Miles City prison cells, just waiting for their trials to start on

Monday."

"Whoa! Monday? I suppose that's the advantage of having a judge living in your community. No need to wait weeks or months for a circuit judge to put in an appearance. I'm glad Bob and the others made it back safely." Blake met Samuel's eyes. "As you know, lawmen have been bushwhacked en route with prisoners and the accused have escaped."

Samuel continued eating without comment.

"Decided when you're leaving?" queried Ernest.

Samuel's head popped up when Blake hadn't replied. "You mean me?"

"You mentioned last night that…" began Blake.

"Haven't received orders yet," interrupted Burton. "I'll send a telegraph explaining the situation here and requesting new instructions. Don't worry about it, Connors. I'm certain you'll hear from headquarters soon enough."

Just then, an enormous explosion rocked the hotel, rattling the wall of windows where the lawmen were seated. One window a few feet away from them cracked, slipped out of the casing, and smashed onto the floor.

"What the hell was that?" Ernest scrambled out of his chair, tipping it over and sending it crashing to the floor.

"Dynamite, unless I miss my guess," added Blake, leaping to his feet.

"Everyone get out in case this ceiling collapses," shouted Ernest as dirt particles drifted downward and landed on patrons.

"I swear the floor beneath my feet moved," exclaimed Blake.

Ernest led the way as all three men charged out of the hotel, mounted up, and rode north down Main Street.

As they passed by the Spirit Creek General Store, Ernest noticed Ronald Waverly standing out front on the sidewalk.

"Sounds like somebody is breaking them bank robbers out of jail!" bellowed Ronald.

"That would be my guess," replied Ernest who observed that two of the four glass storefront windows were broken, a jagged shard remained on the bottom half of one and a long crack ran from one side to the other in the second window. No wonder the storekeeper sounded a little riled.

Blake waved to Ronald. "The prisoners and whoever broke them out of jail might ride by here with guns drawn. Stay inside. And tell any others to get off the streets also."

Ronald waved a quick acknowledgment, turned and high-tailed it, rounding up a couple of customers standing nearby and herding them inside the mercantile also.

The trio of lawmen continued toward the jailhouse, riding their horses full out.

Ernest leapt out of the saddle and tied the reins around the hitching post across the street from the jailhouse. Blake and Samuel followed suit. All three horses nickered and danced nervously as their owners raced into the street.

Coming from the Joker's Wild Saloon, Deputy Donald Jones shoved the drunk he'd just arrested out of his way. "Consider this your lucky day. Go home and sleep it off. And no more fighting."

"I 'sppreciate that, Domald." The drunk staggered across the street and disappeared down an alleyway as the deputy raced toward the other lawmen.

"Was that what I think it was?" Donald arrived at their side, drawing his gun.

Ernest pulled his gun out of the holster and led the others around the back corner of the jailhouse. He stood gaping at the ruins.

"Holy sheep shit!" exclaimed Samuel.

"Couldn't have said it better myself." Blake almost crashed into the other Pinkerton when he stopped in his tracks, pointing his gun skyward to avoid accidently shooting his counterpart.

Ernest grimaced. The scene before them could only be described as total chaos. He couldn't believe his eyes. The entire back corner of the jailhouse where the far cell was located had been blown to smithereens, resulting in knee deep piles of debris. The brick and wood building appeared damaged beyond repair.

Smoke lingered in the air from the dynamite blast and a small fire burned on one side of the building. Ash and dirt hovered in the air. Weapon drawn, Ernest moved around to the right. Blake pointed left and headed toward the corner where the majority of the damage had been done, his weapon in hand. Adrenaline raced through Ernest's body, causing an embarrassing shake of his hand. Hopefully, no one would notice and those who did would understand it wasn't from cowardliness or fright.

"Do you suppose Charlie and Albert are under all that debris?"

yelled Blake.

Ernest shouted back, "I can't tell. I don't see any limbs sticking out. Don't see anything but a pile of splintered wood and broken bricks."

Several citizens milled around gaping at the scene before them. Men talked among themselves, pointing and waving their arms about. Women wailed and called out their husbands' names while small children clung to their mothers' skirts. As loved ones were reunited, the bystanders moved away and headed home.

Without warning one wall groaned and creaked. "Get back!" shouted Ernest as the wooden front wall buckled in on itself and ever so slowly fell over like an inebriated saloon patron losing consciousness.

Ernest joined Blake and they inspected the spot where the cell holding his father and brother used to be.

"Both prisoners could be under all that rubble," speculated Ernest. "But I don't hear anyone calling for help."

"Someone could have rescued them after the blast, but I haven't spotted anyone standing around that resembled them. Most likely, someone aided in their escape. Or, they'd been killed in the blast." Blake met Ernest's eyes.

Hoping to eliminate the latter option, Ernest took several tentative steps forward. Two men appeared with picks and shovels in their hands, having the same idea.

"Ain't nobody under there." A grizzled and hunched old-timer stood several feet away, wrinkled hands hooked around the straps of his suspenders. "I seen three fellers pull two men out."

"Weren't three fellers, only two helped 'em out," disputed another white-haired man of the same vintage.

"Nope. I seen three of them," the first man insisted.

"Then ya need Miss Patterson to teach ya sums. There was two," countered the second fellow.

Blake retraced his steps. "There were two men in that cell. An older fellow and a younger man. They were both taken away?"

"Sure nuff were," agreed the first man.

"Yep. Helped them fellers onto a pair of horses and headed out that way," he pointed to the west. "Two of them."

"I seen three."

The second fellow appeared to tire of the argument but added enthusiastically, "Ya goin' after 'em, sonny?"

"We certainly are," confirmed Ernest. "Those men attempted to rob the bank yesterday."

The one old-timer cackled and slapped the other man's back. Ernest feared they'd ask him if they could come along. He headed for his horse before it crossed their minds.

Just as he rounded the front of the building, a towering cottonwood's roots gave out. Slowly, the tree crashed down onto the jailhouse roof, smashing it completely. "Hell, where'd those fools get that dynamite?"

"I can only guess," muttered Blake, following him into the street.

Men and women stood around in small groups, many visibly shaking. Doc Benjamin moved amongst them, asking if anyone was hurt. Most folks appeared distraught and only a few were answering or even acknowledging the doctor's questions. Ernest didn't notice anyone covered in blood though, just a few scrapes and scratches.

Reverend Gerald stood some feet back from the scene, Bible in hand, silently praying.

Ernest stepped up beside Blake. "I think someone busted them out. They're probably a couple miles from here by now."

"I agree," said Blake. "A bit overdone though. Where's Samuel?"

"Right here," he answered stepping up from behind.

"Let's ride. We should be able to catch up to them." Ernest headed for the hitching post across the street and the others followed.

"Donald! We're going after them. Stay here and help folks clean up this mess." Ernest was accustomed to giving his little brother orders and having them carried out without question. And was especially thankful for it at times like this.

"Will do," Donald called back. "Go get them bastards and bring them back."

"We'll be taking them to Miles City. No sense bringing them back here," said Ernest.

"Oh hell, you're right." Donald grinned, sheepishly. "Guess that's why you're the boss."

Ernest laughed. "Just remember that. We're going to drop by the hotel, get June to pack us some grub, and then head off after the prisoners."

"You'll probably pick up a few volunteers to posse up with you," suggested Donald.

"Any and all help would be welcomed and appreciated." Blake climbed into the saddle.

Just as the men rode off, a man stepped up. "Deputy Jones, you'd better come take a look see at this."

CHAPTER 15

A trail of dust followed the lawmen out of Spirit Creek twenty minutes later. Riding fast and hard, Ernest, Blake and Samuel were joined by Luke Carlyle, Ned Armstrong and Robert Morgan. The threesome, who happened to be palavering at the feed store when the explosion happened, readily volunteered to help in the search. The lawmen appreciated the gesture; they could use all the help they would get. Ernest deputized the lot of them before they headed out of town, traveling west and a bit south.

The posse rode in silence under a blazing high-noon sun for a good hour, intermittently breaking into groups and scouting the area in twos before joining up again.

"I figure you didn't see any sign of them." Ernest pulled his horse alongside Blake.

"Spotted signs of recent travel by horseback but can't say it was them for sure," reported Blake, swiping his shirt sleeve across his damp brow.

Luke chimed in, "Should have brought my cowhand, Wounded Wolf. He worked as a tracker when employed by the government years ago."

"He woulda found 'em by now," offered Ned, Luke's ranch foreman.

A half hour later, the six of them joined up again and stopped beside the Tongue River. "We best give the horses a little drink and let them rest awhile, then head out again," suggested Samuel.

Ernest's stomach grumbled in protest; the explosion had

interrupted his breakfast. "I could eat a little something, too."

For the next twenty minutes, the men chewed down some of the grub they'd acquired at the hotel while they planned their next strategy. Wandering back to the river bank, the men cupped their hands and drank their fill of the cool, swift-moving water before retrieving their rested horses. After tightening cinches, the posse rode off and circled the huge butte that had sheltered them from the brisk wind during their break.

While they'd eaten, menacing clouds had moved in from the west, darkening the sky and partially blocking the sun. As the search continued, the wind increased in velocity, blowing dust and debris into the posse's eyes and mouths. Each man covered the lower portion of his face with his bandana to ease the discomfort. Ernest considered the irony for a second. At the moment, the posse probably resembled bandits as much as the escaped prisoners had during the robbery.

Tracking the prisoners had proven difficult enough under the blazing sun. Squinting through a wall of dust wasn't improving Ernest's mood and he silently cursed the lack of spring rain. Now, he hoped the posse wouldn't receive a dousing before spotting the outlaws. Searching through a downpour wouldn't be any easier and would totally obliterate any tracks.

"Look!" Ernest pointed to the distant horizon where he'd swear he spotted what appeared to be several men on horseback. "Do you see that?"

"Yep. Do you suppose that's them?" replied Blake.

"Could be," said Samuel.

"Let's hope so," added Ned.

Blake pulled a spyglass out of his vest pocket and took a look see. "Can't distinguish anything. Just blurred forms moving in and out of a small cloud of dust."

Luke surveyed the land. "Either we almost overtook them, or the dang fools have been traveling in a semicircle. Do you suppose they know where they are?"

"Maybe their brains are a little addled from that explosion," speculated Ernest.

Ned scoffed, "Or they knows we's searchin' fer 'em and they's tryin' to trip us up."

The posse urged their horses across the parched rangeland in an effort to catch up. The eastern portions of the state were never blessed with the moisture the mountainous western sections received, and the dry ground allowed them to gallop safely in their pursuit. Once again, Ernest hoped the heavens wouldn't open for a while longer, despite the local ranchers' prayers for a good spring rain.

As the posse neared the riders ahead of them, a shot rang out. All six men and their mounts scattered, taking cover behind groupings of nearby bushes.

Samuel blustered, "That answer your question, Ernest?"

Ernest moved his horse up beside Blake's gelding. "Can you wager a guess at how many of them there are?"

"One trigger-happy bastard for sure," reckoned Blake. "Probably my brother. Could be four or five others."

The men remained hidden from sight for several minutes, discussing the best way to proceed.

"Do you suppose they've moved on, or are they circling back to sneak up on us?" questioned Luke.

Judging by the local rancher's calm demeanor even after being shot at, Ernest suspected Luke had ridden with a posse on several occasions in the past. Probably while Ernest himself still occupied a seat in the schoolhouse. "Don't know. But we can't just sit here. Let's head out and see if they start shooting again."

The others nodded in agreement.

"Ernest and I will go first and then wait a minute and see what happens," volunteered Blake, reining his horse around the left side of the bush into the open. Ernest rode around from the other side.

Ernest grimaced when he heard a shot which appeared to whiz by his fellow lawman's ear.

"Dammit," Blake cursed, reining Humbug back behind the bushes.

Ernest skedaddled back as well. "Hell, they're just waiting to pluck us off like sitting ducks."

Blake and Ernest huddled together to devise a plan while Samuel hung back with the others.

"Ned and Samuel, you two will charge out through the middle, firing your pistols and providing cover for me and Luke on the left and Robert and Blake on the right," instructed Ernest. Glancing at the others, he continued, "When we're in position, Ned and Samuel will separate and reload then get back into the thick of it. While we move out, the four of us won't fire unless we have one of them in our sights. Then take turns firing and reloading with your partner, covering each other."

Everyone nodded in understanding.

"And try to work your way around back of them. If we can circle them all the better. We don't want any of them sneaking away. Once we've got them corralled in, watch where you're shooting though. We don't want to hit each other," added Blake.

"We'll be careful," promised Luke. "None of these men are reckless with a gun."

Ernest nodded, "I know."

"Glad to hear it," replied Blake. "I'd say there's no more than six of them, so the odds are even. Choose your targets wisely. Stick your bandanas back on as another way to distinguish them from us. They won't be expecting that."

"Good idea," agreed Robert.

In groups of two, the men separated into the planned pairs while 'good luck' and 'be careful' encouragements were exchanged.

Ernest took a deep breath and blew it out. He spit out the mouthful of dust he'd collected during the discussion a few moments ago, and then pulled his bandana up over his nose. The others adjusted theirs also. He blinked furiously, feeling like a bushel of dust was irritating his eyes. There was no help for it.

"Go", shouted Ernest.

Ned and Samuel burst from behind the grove of cottonwoods, pistols firing, and headed up the middle toward the bushes where the outlaws had taken refuge. The ruse appeared to work. Ned and Samuel fired off several shots before the outlaws' pistols answered. Ernest followed Luke into the fray from the left while Blake and Robert emerged from the right.

* * *

Several bullets missed Blake by mere inches, raising the hairs on his arms. He hunkered down over Humbug's neck, making himself a smaller target. To the horse's credit, he never demonstrated an ounce of nervousness or concern no matter the degree of utter chaos they both found themselves in. And they'd shared some hair-raising experiences together the past five years.

"Good boy," encouraged Blake.

He spotted a man to his left, pistol pointed directly at him. No bandana. Blake fired and the fellow returned fire. He missed Blake by an inch. The fellow's horse turned and headed behind the bushes. Blake couldn't tell if the rider had reined his mount away, or if Blake had hit his target and the horse had been spooked.

Damn. He'd likely missed, but then again, thankfully, so had the outlaw.

A barrage of gunfire continued around him and he straightened in the saddle, searching for another target. The situation was clear: kill or be killed. Hopefully, the outlaws would soon shout a word of surrender, or give up when they were wounded and unable to return fire. Bullets buzzed by him and his left arm smarted as if he'd been stung by a bee. He returned fire in the direction it had come.

Robert's horse sidled up to Humbug, and Robert called to Blake while reloading, "We must have hit a couple of them by now."

"You'd think some of them are wounded, but there doesn't seem to be any let up." Blake fired another round.

"Unless we misjudged their numbers," suggested Robert. He reined his horse in front of Blake and took over while Blake reloaded his pistol.

The shootout continued for several more minutes, amid cursing and shouting from both sides. Suddenly, the shooting ceased and silence reigned over the rangeland.

"Did some escape or did we shoot them all?"

Blake shrugged. "I don't know, Robert. Even if they're only wounded, they might be unable to return fire."

The lawmen moved forward to survey the damages. "I didn't see anyone ride off," observed Ernest who joined them. "What about you?"

"Too busy ducking bullets," admitted Blake. "Dammit. Judging by the gunshots, there seemed to be more than just a half dozen of the buggers."

The posse rode forward, pistols still drawn in case the ceasefire was a trick. Riding behind a cluster of pine trees, Blake discovered his father's body slumped over the man's own horse. Someone must have stolen the animal out of the livery where Blake had arranged for his pa and brother's horses' care after their owners were arrested. "Pa!" he called and received no response. Blake feared the worst. As he moved closer, Humbug danced sideways. Not a good sign.

Robert reined his mount in front of Blake and leaned sideways on his horse. He slowly lifted Charlie Connors's head off the fellow's chest. Blood seeped from a bullet hole in his forehead. "He's dead," Robert confirmed.

Just then, Ernest yelled from several yards away, "Blake, come over here."

As soon as Blake rode up, he noticed three bodies scattered in different directions where they'd fallen to the ground in crumpled heaps. Blake swallowed the bile that rose. No matter how long he did this job, he knew he'd never become accustomed to death.

Albert Connors's sightless eyes stared unseeing at the heavens. His old swaybacked horse stood a few feet away, also sprung from the livery. Knowing the wasted and lawless life his brother had led, Blake doubted he'd be heading heavenward any time soon. More likely, the devil would be welcoming him at this very moment, as well as his pa.

Bullets had buzzed like bees in a field of lavender around everyone's heads during the encounter. Who knew which of the posse's bullets had killed his pa and brother? Hell, the bullets could have been his own. Kill or be killed. He'd chosen this line of work, and he lived with the consequences. Thinking on it, he'd avoided a good many bullets himself. More than anyone else if he wasn't mistaken. Or it could have been his imagination working overtime in the moment.

Just then Ernest and Donald rode up beside him.

"Tell him what you told me," encouraged Ernest.

Donald grimaced. "We found a dead body under the rubble. No one could identify him. He was missing one arm and the rest of him... Well, his own mama couldn't swear to his identity. If someone hired him to detonate the explosive, he overestimated by quite a bit the quantity required for the job."

"His name might have been Marvin something." Blake reined in Humbug who was becoming agitated by the scent of death. "Pa mentioned the cook who traveled with them was good with explosives. Maybe the old fool just was bragging on it. There'll be no proving who the fellow was. We'll have to bury him in a grave marked 'Drifter' I guess."

"If someone comes looking for him, we'll have to explain what happened. Do you recognize the other two lying there, Blake?" inquired Ernest.

"The big fellow on the left rode with a gang I infiltrated a few years back. Escaped during a robbery. Everyone called him Pete, but again, I haven't a clue about a last name," he answered. "Never seen the other man in my life."

"Do you even realize you're bleeding?" Donald stared at him.

Blake's gaze moved to his left arm which had been bothering him a mite. A crimson patch of blood had formed just below his shoulder. "Damn," he swore. "One of those bullets must have grazed me."

"I don't doubt it," blurted Robert who'd been riding alongside the Pinkerton. "Thought I'd been dropped into a damn war zone for a while there. Seemed, for some reason, everyone was shooting at us."

"More specifically, shooting at me. Appears word has gotten out who I work for. I'd wager all of these fellows wanted me dead, including my family. Pa never took kindly to anyone crossing him." Blake grimaced as he held his clean handkerchief to the wound, applying pressure to staunch the bleeding. It hurt like the dickens but soon the bleeding appeared to stop.

Ernest straightened in the saddle, stretching his back. "Luke lit out for Wilber Simpson's ranch over yonder. He figured he'd lend us a wagon to haul these bodies back to Spirit Creek. Ned headed back to town to inform the mayor that the escaped prisoners were dead, and there wasn't any cause for concern that the buggers would appear back in town with folks unprotected."

"That accounts for everyone but Samuel. Where the hell is he?" Blake glanced behind him as if expecting him to be hiding there.

"Ain't seen him," said Robert.

"Me either," added Ernest.

Donald shrugged. "Wasn't here when I rode up and he wasn't with Ned when I crossed paths with him."

Blake felt himself pale, and not from loss of blood. "Do you suppose he's been wounded, too? Or worse?"

"Search the area. Yell if you find him." Ernest reined his horse around and rode south.

Blake headed west, Robert north, and Donald to the east. Of course, the clouds passed and the sun came out now that all the shooting was over. Not a drop of rain had fallen yet again. The ranchers wouldn't like that. Dry grassland didn't feed cattle and there was added risk of lightning strikes starting prairie grass fires. At least, it made searching the area for Burton a mite easier.

An hour later, the men met back beside the bodies where Luke and Wilber were loading the deceased into the back of a large supply wagon. Blake overheard mutterings about fellows making poor choices and wasting lives.

"Since I didn't hear anyone yelling or firing off his pistol, I assume none of you found anything." Ernest removed his hat and scratched his head. He shoved his Stetson back on and reached for the reins hung loosely over his horse's neck.

"Nothing," said Robert and Donald in unison.

"Saw some blood on the ground a ways off." Blake shifted in the saddle and pointed toward the dead men. "But it could have come from one of these fellows before he dropped."

"Where do you suppose Burton went?" asked Donald.

Blake rubbed his jaw. "I don't know, but there was something off about that man. Acted plenty strange for a Pinkerton. Can't put my finger on anything specific. Just troubled me a bit, him showing up here without any forewarning."

Luke stepped up to Blake. "I found this on the ground on my way back from Wilber's place. Caught the sunlight, otherwise I wouldn't have noticed. Thought it strange." He handed Blake the shiny metal detective's badge Samuel had shown them the day he arrived in Spirit Creek.

"Now, *that* is damn strange. An agent wouldn't part with his badge except at gunpoint. Even then I'd be a bit reluctant," admitted Blake.

"All ready," called Wilber seated on the wagon bench, reins in hand. "We're burnin' daylight."

"Let's go. I believe this Samuel Burton fellow, if that's even his real name, disappeared on purpose. Something isn't right here." Blake reined his horse around and led the way back to town.

For the next hour, Blake rode in silence while he digested all that had happened today. The explosion. The pursuit of the escaped prisoners. His pa and brother's deaths. The disappearance of the fellow he'd silently questioned whether or not was a fellow Pinkerton. Now he hadn't any doubts about the latter. He'd risk Humbug in a wager that the man was an imposter.

What troubled him most, he hadn't the slightest urge to mourn his deceased family members. Was his brother's caustic attitude toward him and his father's deplorable treatment of him, especially as a child, responsible for how Blake felt? Or had working in law-enforcement all these years, seeing the worst of mankind, hardened his heart more than he would have ever suspected?

Perhaps he should retire after all.

CHAPTER 16

During reading time in her classroom, Ivy heard the explosion and the floor of the ancient schoolhouse shuddered beneath her feet. The children screamed and everyone streamed out of the schoolhouse fearing the old walls would crumble down around them.

Amid the commotion, Ivy noticed a cloud of dust or smoke or both rising skyward in the direction of the jailhouse. She realized immediately what happened. Someone broke her family out of their jail cell.

"No," she whispered. "Pa, what have you done?"

"Did you say something, Miss Patterson?"

"Just talking to myself, sweetheart." Ivy patted the little girl's back. "Don't worry."

Several children stood wide-eyed while others sniffled quietly.

"Children, I want everyone to remain here until your parents come to fetch you," instructed Ivy.

The students nodded in understanding and huddled in groups on the grassy schoolyard ground. Some of the youngest ones who didn't comprehend the seriousness of the situation entertained themselves in a game of tag.

One by one, the students were collected by their parents, and soon Ivy found herself alone. Did she dare show up at the jailhouse? What had happened to her pa and brother? Was Blake there with Ernest?

"How are you holding up?" The familiar female voice startled her from her musings.

"Aunt Minnie! Have you heard anything?"

"Come inside and make me a cup of tea. I'll tell you everything I know." Her aunt wandered through the classroom, following Ivy into her quarters.

Within an hour, the teapot emptied, as did the plate of oatmeal cookies Ivy had set out.

"So, we just wait until the lawmen return to town," mumbled Ivy to herself.

Aunt Minnie rose from the chair and grabbed her wrap off the small cot. "Not on your life, young lady. I intend to be there when Blake returns. I want to hear the entire story in detail. How dare that fool Charlie arrange his escape? Blasted out of jail with dynamite of all things. Any number of passersby could have been injured or killed. He's getting a good tongue lashing the minute I set eyes on that man."

Ivy agreed with her aunt's heated words and strong conviction. What had her pa and brother been thinking? They hadn't changed one bit since the night she'd escaped from them and their despicable lifestyle. Selfish men. Thinking only of themselves and hang the safety of anyone else.

As Ivy and her aunt approached the jailhouse, a commotion took place outside the blacksmith's shop where a supply wagon was parked outside the side door that the undertaker used for his coffin-making business. Someone had been killed and the body returned to town to be fitted for a box for burial.

But who?

Ivy reached for her aunt's hand. "Please, Aunt Minnie, it can't be Ernest. Or Blake. Anyone but them."

"We'll learn who it was soon enough. A little prayer won't hurt in the meantime," encouraged her aunt, matching Ivy's stride.

Mayor Barker stepped up beside them. "Ivy, should you be here? Have you heard?"

Ivy's eyes filled with tears. "Ernest?" she whispered.

"Lord, no. Oh, my dear, I didn't mean to frighten you like that. But…" The mayor reached for her hand, appearing to hesitate a moment.

Ivy braced herself. "Just tell me."

"Your pa and brother were killed along with a few other fellows who'd helped them escape," explained the mayor. "The man who'd detonated the blast died also, overestimated the requirements to do the job."

Ivy sighed heavily.

"So Ernest and Blake are all right?" Aunt Minnie appeared to be holding her breath.

"Yes, ma'am, they accompanied the bodies back to town. Arrived about fifteen minutes ago."

* * *

Blake stepped across the street and approached his sister and aunt, a beautiful sight. Both of them smiling at him, no doubt happy to see him safe and sound. And he was thankful to be in one piece considering all he'd endured during the encounter with the escaped prisoners and their cronies. The outcome for him could have been so different had one of their bullets found its mark. His sister and aunt would have been devastated, but fortunately, the law-enforcements gods had watched over him.

Aunt Minnie wrapped him in her arms, squeezed him tightly and then stepped back. "Let me look at you." Her gaze roamed over him like a warm caress. "My word, you're bleeding, boy!"

"Not anymore." Blake gently touched his arm and inspected the blood-stained shirt sleeve. "A bullet grazed my shoulder, but I'll be fine."

Ivy reached for his hand and pulled him up onto the sidewalk. "You're going to Doc Benjamin's clinic this minute. I won't have you dying, too."

"I'm not dying." Blake allowed his sister to drag him along in the direction he'd been heading anyway. "I'm going to the telegraph office to..."

"Not until…"

"No, little sister. We're going there first," insisted Blake, intent on his mission. "I need to send off a warning to Sheriff Sanders that someone might try breaking the Bailey gang out of jail, too. We don't need more lives in danger, more prisoners being killed."

Ivy dropped her brother's hand and strode alongside him as he turned at the corner and walked toward the telegraph office. Aunt Minnie tripped along behind them in an effort to keep up with the much younger folk. Blake stopped and took her arm, preventing a fall.

"Thank you, son," she gasped, puffing from the exertion. "I'm not accustomed to participating in a foot race."

"I'm sorry," apologized Blake. "But every minute counts."

Ivy waved her brother ahead and hooked her hand around her aunt's arm. "Go. We'll be along soon."

Blake raced ahead, his long-legged stride delivering him to the telegraph building's door in no time. He approached the old telegraph operator and tapped the fellow's counter, impatiently. "I need to send a couple of telegraphs right now."

"All right, sonny. What ya need to say?"

Ten minutes later, Blake appeared back on the sidewalk, closing the telegraph office door behind himself, just as his aunt and sister arrived. "It's done. I just pray my warning arrives in time. And I also sent a telegraph to my superiors in Chicago advising them of the outcome here. Dang it, I forgot to mention that Samuel Burton disappeared during the shootout." Perhaps his mind wasn't working at full capacity considering the blood he'd lost and the shoulder pain he'd been attempting to ignore.

"Disappeared?" blurted Ivy.

"When the dust cleared, there was no sign of him. He'd just up and left. I'm not certain he was even a Pinkerton agent since Luke Carlyle found the badge he'd been waving around out on the range. I believe he was here under false pretenses," speculated Blake.

"Why would he create such a sham?" Aunt Minnie paled, pointing to Blake's injured arm. "Did that young devil come here intent on doing you harm?"

"I'm not certain," admitted Blake.

"You don't suppose someone would do the same thing in Miles City, do you? Try to blow up their jailhouse?" Aunt Minnie wrung her hands.

"I honestly don't know," replied Blake. "But I'm hoping my telegraph serves as a warning."

"I can hardly believe it happened here." Ivy shook her head. "Can hardly believe Pa and Albert are dead, although I've expected for years to receive word at any time of all your deaths. But I certainly never suspected you worked with the Pinkerton folks."

Blake rubbed his sister's arms tenderly. "The news about Pa and Albert is still a shock though, isn't it?"

Ivy just nodded.

"We'll bury them, mourn the loss awhile, and then move on," Aunt

Minnie assured her kin.

Blake stood hands on hips. "So, who's accompanying me to the doctor's office? If I recall correctly, he works out of his house."

"Yes, he does, at old Doc Fitzgerald's mansion. Let's go. Even if there isn't a bullet in your arm, I don't want you to get infection." Ivy reached for her brother's hand and led him toward Doc's home. Aunt Minnie hooked her arm around his uninjured arm and followed.

"I cannot tell you how proud I am of you, young man." Aunt Minnie beamed like a proud mother. "I raised your sister, but I'm so happy you've also found your way. Leading a law-abiding and productive life."

"Thank you." Blake leaned over and kissed his aunt's cheek. "We're a family of three honest citizens now, and I pray we've seen the end of the lawless-living Connors legacy."

"Amen," stated Aunt Minnie. "A lawman and a schoolteacher. I couldn't have hoped for a better nephew and niece."

The threesome strode up the wooden stairs at Doc Benjamin's side entrance, leading to his clinic. Blake rapped loudly on the wooden door and called, "Anyone home?"

Within a few seconds, Doc Benjamin appeared wearing a white shirt rolled to the elbows under a waistcoat. "What have we got here?" he asked, wiping his hands on a towel and speaking through the screened door. His woolen trousers were flecked with water and Blake speculated that perhaps he'd been washing medical equipment.

Blake sighed. "Had a run-in with a stray bullet."

"I'm assuming the bullet won?"

"Just a graze, but my womenfolk insist I get it tended to."

"Wise ladies indeed. Come on in." Doc directed them into the clinic, leaving the ladies seated on the waiting-to-hear sofa while leading Blake toward an examination room. "Heard you'd had a bit of excitement today. Hopefully, the town builds another jailhouse soon. With more and more drifters passing through, and more saloons opening to accommodate the ever-increasing population, we'll be needing a new jail sooner than later."

"My thoughts, too," agreed Blake through clenched teeth as the doctor peeled his shirt away, exposing the bloody wound. "I'll help Ernest organize a build."

"Just grazed you by the looks of it," observed Doc. "But pieces of your shirt and a peck of dirt are stuck in there. I need to clean out the wound and then flush it good with alcohol. Hopefully, there won't be too much infection."

Doc guided Blake toward an examination table. "Hop up there and lay your head on the pillow. Let me get a good look at that wound."

Blake grimaced while the doctor poked and prodded the site. "I'm just pleased that I lived to feel that hot poker you're stabbing in there."

"Sorry, no poker but this is going to hurt. Probably more than getting nicked by that bullet in the first place."

Blake blinked rapidly to discourage the black spots floating before his eyes. Lying down proved worse than standing on his feet. Damn if he would pass out while being administered to though. At least, not if he could help it.

Doc lit a lantern and moved it into the most advantageous position before he started digging debris out of the wound. Blake clamped his eyes shut and concentrated on the day's success instead of the pain. Once again, he'd cheated death during a dangerous assignment. Someone upstairs had watched out for him today, and he just prayed his luck wouldn't run out before he could retire. A groan escaped his lips. "If this doctoring thing doesn't pan out, you could work as a wartime torture expert."

Doc ignored the comment and kept at his mission. He'd probably heard worse complaints. Blake grimaced one last time before everything went black.

Blake pried his eyes open sometime later and blinked in the bright lamplight. He discovered Doc piling up medical instruments on a white towel lying alongside himself on the bed. Doc scooped up the towel and set it on a table across the room. "Almost done. Just needs some cleansing."

"How long have I been out?"

"Almost a half hour." Doc returned, holding a large bottle of alcohol. "Don't think you're concussed though. Probably just from the pain."

Blake braced himself as Doc poured alcohol over and into the wound. "Dang it, Doc, that hurts." He gritted his teeth, almost leaping off the table. His arm could have been ripped off and it wouldn't have hurt as much.

"I appreciate your verbal restraint," said Doc. "Most patients' language is a mite colorful at this point."

Blake blew out his breath when Doc replaced the stopper in the bottle of alcohol. "Let's not do that again," he suggested.

"Not tonight anyway." Doc applied a clean bandage to the wound. "Don't suppose I can convince you to stay here overnight?"

"Not a chance." Blake sat up slowly, climbed down off the table, and followed Doc along the hallway leading back to the waiting area. Thankfully, the spots in front of his eyes had disappeared and the dizziness lessened. "I need to check in with Ernest in case we receive news from Miles City that their prisoners escaped and Sanders and his men need our help."

Ivy gasped, overhearing Blake's words. "You're not going anywhere except back to the hotel to rest!"

Doc and Blake exchanged a look.

"She's a wise young lady. You should listen to her advice," suggested Doc.

"All right. We'll check in with Ernest and then I'll return to my room and rest until I hear I'm needed," conceded Blake.

Doc handed Ivy a bundle. "Here's some laudanum for pain and sufficient bandage material to last a couple of days. If he develops a fever, bring him back here kicking and screaming if necessary."

"I promise," said Ivy, smiling. "I'll enlist Ernest and Donald's help if he doesn't cooperate."

Blake frowned. "I was happier when I didn't have a sister nagging me."

"Get accustomed to it, big brother. I'm not going anywhere."

CHAPTER 17

Sunday, May 15, 1892

Blake wandered into The Spirit Creek Hotel's dining room, thankful he'd been able to convince his sister to allow him to sleep unsupervised in his own room last night. After promising to send for their Aunt Minnie should he start feeling poorly, Blake had sighed in relief the moment Ivy headed home to the schoolhouse, leaving him in peace.

His shoulder throbbed like the dickens and his head still swam from the healthy swig of laudanum he'd resorted to in the wee hours before finally falling asleep. But he'd live. What more could he ask for?

"Hey, Connors, over here," called Ernest, seated at a window table with Donald.

Blake noticed the broken window had been repaired and the dust and debris had been cleaned up. The female hotel owner seemed quite conscientious about her business. He joined his colleagues, slumping into a chair across from Ernest. Blake had washed and changed his clothes, even brushed his teeth, but his body ached as if he'd been run over by a few dozen stampeding Longhorns.

"You look like hell," observed Ernest, sipping a cup of coffee.

Blake grimaced. "Thank you so much for noticing."

Donald chuckled. "You saw Doc. Did you need much sewing up?"

"Doc cleaned out the wound and then in my estimate dumped in at least a gallon of alcohol before bandaging it. Don't believe there was stitching up involved, but I passed out for a time. My head's still a little foggy." Blake blew out his breath. "Just happy to be here to share breakfast with you fellows."

Ernest whistled low. "With all the bullets flying, I wasn't certain any of us would live to see today, but we ended up on the winning side."

Donald nodded. "Better than the alternative."

Gertie appeared at the table, coffee pot in hand. "Blake, would you like some coffee? I heard you were hurt something awful yesterday, that some outlaw shot you. I'm just so thankful you're all right. You are all right? You're sitting here and all so…"

"Whoa! I'm doing fair to middling, but I'll survive," reported Blake, smiling at her concern. He would never admit it to Ernest or Donald, but it felt good having a female worrying about him. He could get used to it, given half a chance.

"Bring us all plates of eggs, sausage, potatoes, whatever you've got, Gertie." Ernest smiled at the waitress. "Old Blake here is going to live so just go about your work and don't worry about his sorry hide."

Gertie glared at the sheriff. "It ain't against the law to worry about someone."

"No it isn't and I'm certain Blake appreciates your concern. But we've got business to discuss and it requires privacy." Ernest watched Gertie's reluctant departure.

"Sounds serious," said Blake, watching Gertie's swaying hips as she headed to the kitchen.

"Not really. Just figured you didn't need a dang female hovering over you," confided Ernest.

Blake leaned back in his chair. "Thought you didn't believe in little white lies. I can think of worse things to greet a man's day than a pretty girl expressing concern for him."

Ernest scowled. "To each his own."

"You should let my sister worry about you again. Might lead to you two patching up your differences," suggested Blake.

Donald choked on a mouthful of coffee.

Ernest glared at the Pinkerton. "There's no chance of that happening."

Blake waited for him to expound on the statement, but no additional words were forthcoming.

"You're a dang fool. My sister loved you unconditionally, and then you up and broke her heart."

Ernest leaned back and glared at Blake.

He continued, "I'd trade places with you in a second. Being a Pinkerton detective, especially one who works undercover, can be a damn lonely job. Certainly not the glamorous life the dime novels make it out to be."

"Never said it was. Just mentioned I'd considered it at one time." Ernest shifted position in his chair.

Gertie appeared at the table and distributed plates heaped with eggs, sausages and biscuits. "Do you need more coffee?"

"In a minute," said Blake, smiling at her.

Gertie hurried off toward the kitchen.

Blake leaned across the table. "You've found the perfect girl to spend the rest of your life with, and you're throwing it all away. I only wish I could find the time for such a thing."

Donald laughed. "I know one candidate who would readily volunteer."

Blake tossed one of his biscuits at his head.

Donald's hand snatched it out of the air and he took a bite.

"Ernest needs to realize what he's throwing away." Blake tucked into his breakfast. His stomach had been grumbling for a half hour already. Apparently, getting yourself shot gave a fellow a powerful appetite.

"Even if he knows, he's too stubborn to admit it," suggested Donald, forking eggs into his mouth.

"Well, there isn't a sweeter girl in the entire world than my little sister. She's exactly like our mother was: kind-hearted, generous, caring, loving. Nothing like our heartless, selfish father who only looked for ways to steal what he wanted. The man never did an honest day's work in his entire miserable life."

Blake paused for a sip of coffee and then continued, "Ivy didn't tell you who she really was, but I can't blame her one bit. I hated riding with my pa and his kind, even knowing I was doing it on the right side of the law. When Ivy lit out days after Ma's passing, I wanted to go fetch her. Pa grumbled about it and said she'd be back in a day or two. When I realized she wasn't returning, he forbade me to go look for her. Slandered my sister with a number of names. Ingrate is about the only one suitable for repeating in a public place. Pa sounded more upset that he'd lost a cook and housekeeper than a daughter."

Ernest thumped the table with his fist. "Don't change the fact Ivy lied to an entire town."

Donald chimed in, "For Pete's sake, Ernest, so she told a fib because she was too embarrassed to admit who her family was. Does that mean you'll forever condemn her for it?"

Ernest didn't answer.

"Well, I'm just saying you're an idiot if you let my sister get away." Blake pushed his chair back from the table and lit a cigar. "That's it. I'm not saying another word on the matter."

"Well, I agree with you, Blake." Donald glared at his brother. "Seems like somebody had better do some serious thinking before it's too late. Perhaps ask for some divine guidance while listening to the reverend's sermon later this morning."

Ernest leapt up from the table, catching his chair before it toppled over. He tossed a few coins on the table before charging out the door.

"Suppose that went as well as could be expected. Want to wager what happens first? My shoulder heals or your brother proposes again?" asked Blake.

"A dollar on your shoulder," bet Donald.

* * *

Ernest rushed out of the hotel dining room before he blurted something he'd regret. Seemed a fellow couldn't break an engagement with good reason, without everybody and his dog having an opinion on it.

Dang it all, Ivy lied to him!

He strode down the wooden sidewalk headed for his office in the jailhouse. There'd be the dickens to pay when his mother noticed he'd skipped out on Sunday services today. But he wasn't up to answering questions or enduring stares and glares from every female in town. No doubt, the fairer set would take Ivy's side in the matter.

After a moment, he halted in his tracks. The damn jailhouse was nothing more than an enormous pile of burnt lumber and broken bricks, and it would take a dozen men to remove the tree from what had been the roof. The realization that he no longer had an office struck him like a punch to the gut. So where the hell was he going?

"Hell and damnation!" Ernest turned on his heel and walked toward home.

Perhaps he'd use the kitchen in the little cottage he rented from Luke Carlyle for an office until a new jailhouse could be built. While the fellows tore down the building's remains, he needed to stuff what they could find of his files and paperwork into boxes. He doubted there would be much to find. And what would he do for a cell if it proved necessary to arrest a drunk or two on a Saturday night? He couldn't just lock the inebriated fools in the pantry!

Ernest took the steps to his cabin two at a time, charged inside, and slammed the door closed. "This is all those damned Connors fools' fault." He cursed the sorry excuses for human beings that had occupied the cell, while hanging his Stetson on the hook by the back door.

Ernest stood in the kitchen, contemplating his next move. He thrust his hands into his denim pockets. His breath caught when his fingers encircled the ruby engagement ring he'd stuck in there and then totally forgotten about. He felt himself paling with the realization it could have fallen out during the pursuit of the prisoners and the shootout that followed. He could have lost it any number of times, but he hadn't. Did that mean fate intended for the ring to be returned to Ivy's finger?

"Even fate believes I'm in the wrong here."

Ernest spent the better part of the morning contemplating his next move, and not just relating to his job as sheriff.

CHAPTER 18

Saturday, May 21, 1892

Ivy grabbed a towel, pulled the batch of sweet buns from the woodstove's oven, and set the pan to cool alongside the others on the wooden table. The aroma of cinnamon and brown sugar wafted through her small living quarters, triggering a childhood memory of Saturday mornings when her mother would bake bread and buns and cakes.

She tossed the tea towel aside and slumped onto one of the rickety chairs. Whenever she felt troubled or stressed, she baked. The Jones children gobbled up whatever goodies she dropped by their home, but now she hadn't that luxury. Whatever would she do with all this food?

"How I wish you hadn't died, Ma, and you were here with me," she whispered aloud. "I've made such a mess of everything. What am I going to do?"

Ivy knew now how foolish she'd been to believe her lies would never be revealed. What a ninny she'd been! Risking her job as schoolteacher, her position in the community, and her acceptance by Ernest's family. Most importantly, risking her relationship with Ernest. She'd lost it all. Well, she still hadn't heard from Mr. Waverly to learn if he intended to withdraw his offer to hire her for the next school year.

Was it just a matter of time? Perhaps she should just resign and save herself the humiliation of being dismissed. She could return to California with Aunt Minnie. Perhaps someday replace the aging schoolteacher in Sandy Point and live out her years as a lonely spinster like her aunt. Exactly the dismal future she deserved after lying to everyone.

"Hello! Is anyone home?" called a familiar voice.

"Sadie, I'm in the back," answered Ivy, rising to her feet. At least, she'd donned a clean dress and fixed her hair properly while the last batch of buns was baking.

Ivy smiled as Sadie waddled into the room. "Goodness, are you ever going to have that baby?" she teased.

"He is due next week. And believe me his arrival can't be too soon for me." Sadie lowered herself onto a chair and sighed aloud.

Ivy tipped her head. "He? What makes you think it's a boy?"

"A little girl would never cause her mama all this heartburn and back ache." Sadie grinned. "It must be a boy."

Ivy laughed for the first time in ages. "Would you like a cinnamon bun? Fresh-baked this morning."

Sadie gazed across the assorted offerings cooling on the table and wagged a finger at Ivy. "What's wrong? Only one thing explains all this baking. You're troubled about something. Out with it."

Ivy hated the fact her friend knew her so well. And evading the issue seemed total folly. Sadie would drag the truth out of her one way or another. "I'm certain you've learned by now that everything I told folks about myself has been proven a lie."

Sadie frowned. "With my time so near, my husband refuses to tell me anything he believes will upset me. If I didn't look out the window, I wouldn't even have a clue about the weather."

"So you haven't heard about the attempted bank robbery?"

Sadie gasped. "A bank robbery?"

"Last Friday. Two of the men who tried to rob it were my pa and my older brother."

"But that's impossible. You're an orphan." Sadie met Ivy's eyes and then Ivy's implications registered. "Oh…"

"I've always hated that my pa and brothers were unapologetic bank robbers, proud of their thieving reputations." Ivy wrung her hands. "When I sent in my letter of application, I never mentioned my past. And when I first arrived in town I told anyone who inquired about my family that I was an orphan."

"Yes, you did."

"I escaped from my pa and brothers years ago shortly after my mother died. I tried to erase them from my life, from my memory. I told everyone that I was alone in the world and as far as I was concerned, except for the aunt who raised me, I was. Except for her, I never wanted to lay eyes on the lot of them again."

"When did they arrive here?"

Ivy spent the next half hour explaining the entire story. Sadie interrupted with a barrage of questions which Ivy answered completely, no matter how painful. Ivy held back her tears, knowing she'd probably lost the best friend she'd ever made. But Ivy intended to leave town shortly anyway and Sadie deserved to hear the truth.

"And now they're all dead. Except for the brother who worked for the Pinkerton agency," summarized Sadie.

"He still does, far as I know."

"Well, you can be proud of him for that," suggested Sadie.

"And I am," agreed Ivy, brushing her hair out of her eyes with her hand. "But I haven't a clue what my future holds."

Sadie gasped, noticing her friend's bare finger. "Where's your beautiful ring?"

"About that," whispered Ivy, her voice catching. "When Ernest heard the truth, he called off the engagement. I returned his ring."

"Oh, Ivy, no!" Sadie reached for her hand.

"It's for the best."

"Best, my foot. Give Ernest a little time to digest everything that happened. He loves you so much, he'll come to his senses and ask you to marry him again. I know he will."

"Sadie, if only that were true. But I've hurt him so deeply. If you'd seen the shocked expression on his face and the hurt in his eyes. It's definitely over between us. I lied to him, and that is something he can never forgive."

"But you lied from a sense of survival. You knew people would judge you unfairly because of your kin. Goodness, after the truth became known about my father embezzling funds from his own bank, I thought I'd die from the shame. But now I know that his crimes didn't reflect on me at all." Sadie patted Ivy's hand.

Ivy touched her head. "Up here, what you're saying makes sense. In my heart, I can't bring myself to believe it, and neither should you."

A pain-filled expression appeared on Sadie's face, and Ivy braced herself for the inevitable. Here it comes. Her best friend intended to disown her. And she had no one to blame but herself.

"Oh goodness, ouch," whispered Sadie, grimacing.

Ivy looked deep into Sadie's eyes, seeing something more than disappointment in a friend. Something definitely was wrong. "What is it?"

"It feels like someone stuck a knife in my lower back. I don't know…" Sadie stood and gasped as a puddle appeared on the floor between her feet.

"Sadie, your water broke!" exclaimed Ivy, leaping off her chair. "Oh my, oh my. You're pains have started! Goodness, what do we do? You're going to have the baby!"

"Hush, Sadie. I'm not having the baby this very minute." Sadie stepped over the puddle and waddled toward the door. "Help me into the carriage and take me to Doc's clinic, please."

Ivy hurried to Sadie's side and carefully guided her down the schoolhouse steps. "Help me, please. Sadie's pains have started," called Ivy to the driver who was smoking a cigar while leaning against the carriage's rear wheel.

Sadie moaned and almost doubled over.

"Tarnation." The man turned as white as a bed sheet, dropped his smoke and ground it out with his boot. One trembling hand held the carriage door open while Ivy helped Sadie inside. The carriage dipped as the fellow leapt onto the driver's bench.

The carriage and its occupants arrived at the clinic in record time.

"If that ride didn't bring that baby into the world, I don't know what will," complained Ivy, glaring at the driver. "I feared she'd be thrown to the floor when you careened around that last turn."

"Sorry, miss." The driver swallowed hard. "I was just afraid that…"

"Never mind. Help me inside or I will birth this child right here," threatened Sadie, bending forward and holding her swollen middle.

"Oh no you won't," ordered Ivy, helping her friend up the stairs leading to Doc's clinic. "I absolutely forbid such a thing."

As they entered, Doc's wife, Pearl Johnson, glanced up from behind the metal desk occupying the far corner. Ivy ignored the strong antiseptic smell she hated so much, recalling the agonizing hours spent at another doctor's clinic and her mother's unexpected death.

Pearl raced across the floor and reached for Sadie's arm. "Let me help you. It appears we're about to bring Spirit Creek's newest citizen into the world."

Ivy heaved a sigh, grateful to place her friend in the nurse's capable hands. "I'll wait right here, Sadie," she declared as Doc's wife guided the new mother-to-be down the hallway.

"Please have someone send word to Chance for me," requested Sadie through gritted teeth.

"Oh, yes, of course." Ivy raced out the door and crashed into Sadie's driver, pacing the wooden veranda.

"What is it, miss?" he blurted.

"Please return to the ranch and tell Chance that Sadie's pains have started and she's with Doc at the clinic," instructed Ivy.

"Right away, miss. Should have thought of that myself." He leapt aboard the carriage, settled himself on the bench seat, and reined the team of horses back into the street. The rig disappeared from sight at the corner.

Ivy sucked in a deep breath of crisp spring air. The sun beat down overhead. Almost noon. How long would it be before the baby made an appearance? She'd heard that first babies could take hours, but she stepped back inside and flopped down on the waiting-to-hear sofa, prepared to stay as long as it took. She lay down and tucked herself into a comfortable position.

"At least, there's one good thing coming out of this week's turmoil." Having slept little since returning Ernest's ring, Ivy soon drifted off, secretly hoping the baby would be a little girl.

CHAPTER 19

Sunday, May 22, 1892

Ernest tied his horse's reins to the hitching post outside the schoolyard fence. He glanced down the street, first in one direction and then the other. Showing up on the schoolmarm's doorstep at the crack of dawn would appear unseemly to most citizens, unless of course he could use the 'official business' excuse. Somehow, the purpose of this visit didn't come close to qualifying in that regard. He simply needed to talk to Ivy.

She hadn't been at home last night when he'd dropped by. A fact which troubled him most of his sleepless night. Had she been out for a carriage ride with another fellow? Visiting a friend? She could have packed up and left town for all he knew. He swallowed hard. Hopefully, she hadn't eloped with another man!

"Now you're just being foolish," he scolded himself aloud. With Ivy's reputation for responsibility and levelheadedness, she wouldn't have even considered such a thing.

Would she?

Ernest pounded on the schoolhouse door in case Ivy slept quite soundly. When he received no response, he cracked open the still unlocked door, same as he discovered last night.

"Anyone home?" he called, feeling himself pale. What if she'd fallen? Hit her head? He hadn't thought to check her living quarters last night. Good Lord, what if she'd lain injured and unconscious on the floor all night!

Ernest dashed through the classroom and charged into Ivy's room. Empty. An assortment of baked goods occupied the table, uncovered. That wasn't like Ivy to leave food out. Were there mice in the schoolhouse? Obviously not, or they would have enjoyed a feast.

Nothing appeared disturbed. Assorted dresses and shawls hung from a corner rack attached to the walls. He sighed aloud. At least, she hadn't left town.

"Ivy Patterson, where are you?" he muttered aloud.

Ernest returned to the front entryway and flopped down outside on the top step to wait for her.

* * *

Ivy headed for home with leaden feet minutes after the sun began its ascent. She'd never experienced such all-consuming fatigue in her entire life. She'd only managed a couple hours of shuteye, and then she'd helped Chance wear out the rugs in the clinic waiting room.

Thankfully, it was Sunday. Exhausted from the night spent either pacing or slumped on the old sofa, she couldn't have taught today for any amount of money. Her right hip still stung from lying unawares on the rogue spring for the short time she had slept.

But news of the baby's safe arrival shortly after five o'clock this morning warmed her heart. Sadie had presented Chance with a brand new daughter, naming her Abigail after her late mother.

Head hung low, Ivy didn't notice the visitor occupying her front step until she started up the gravel path from the gate.

"What are you doing here?" she blurted, too tired to offer an apology for her rudeness.

Ernest leapt to his feet, stood hands on hips. "Never mind what I'm doing here. Where in blazes have you been? I spent half the night worrying about you, imagining all manner of things that could have happened."

Ivy sighed heavily. "I took Sadie to Doc's clinic yesterday afternoon when her labor pains started. I stayed there all night waiting for the baby to arrive."

Ernest removed his Stetson and scratched his head. "I assume the stork took his own sweet time about it."

"Sadie delivered a healthy baby girl about an hour ago. Abigail Elisa Maxwell is the sweetest little sprout you've ever seen," said Ivy, feeling herself beaming with pride, and Sadie was referring to her as Aunt Ivy already.

"So mother and baby are both doing well."

"Sadie is exhausted but you couldn't wipe the smile off her face if you tried." Ivy stepped around Ernest and entered the schoolhouse. "I'm so tired I can hardly stand and all I did was keep the father-to-be calm. Doc needs to replace the flooring in the waiting room from our pacing."

Ernest smiled and Ivy's heart hurt as she gazed at him. How she would miss his smile, his sheepish grin when she caught him snagging a cookie off the plate, his robust laugh at someone's joke. "Why *are* you here?" she repeated her earlier inquiry, hearing the emotion in her voice.

"We need to talk. I don't feel comfortable being alone with you in your room here. Wouldn't want to provide fodder for the gossips. I know you're tired, but would you consider accompanying me for a short walk?" An optimistic expression accompanied his question.

Ivy cringed inwardly. The thought of taking a casual stroll after spending a mostly sleepless night at the clinic seemed more like punishment than pleasure. "You made your opinion of me well known. I don't imagine there's much to talk over, and I'm about to drop in my tracks. Couldn't we take a walk this evening? Perhaps after supper sometime?" she suggested.

"No, Ivy, I need to talk to you now."

"All right. All right." Ivy turned and headed out the door. She tripped on the bottom step, but Ernest's strong arms reached out and encircled her waist before she fell. "Thank you," she whispered, her head throbbing with a headache from lack of sleep.

Ernest released his grip on her middle and reached for her hand instead. Five minutes later, they entered the Grayson Gardens Park. Soon, Ivy found herself standing beside the park bench where her beloved had proposed several weeks ago. Tears filled her eyes with the memory. Why had he brought her here? To rub in her face the fact that he no longer loved her? To scold her yet again for lying to him?

Ernest kissed the back of her hand. "Sweetheart, I can see the unshed tears in your eyes. Please don't cry." He reached up and brushed away the lone tear that had trickled down her cheek.

"I'm sorry," Ivy whispered, sniffling softly. How could he expect her to stand here and not shed a tear for all that they'd lost? For everything that could have been had she not lied?

"I've spent a great deal of time thinking about what you did. The deceptions. How I reacted when I first learned about it. Blake and Ernest expressed their opinions on my breaking off our engagement. I contemplated what I did, what I said to you."

Ivy met his eyes. She couldn't read his expression. Was he trying to tell her he'd fallen out of love with her because of what she'd done? Or was he simply apologizing for his explosive words? Meeting for a final goodbye? She swiped away her tears, refusing to let him see how badly he'd hurt her. She just wanted to crawl into her bed, toss the covers over her head, and ignore the world and everyone in it.

"I need to apologize to you. I realize now that my male ego can withstand a bruising. In my line of work, I'm always covered in bruises from wrestling with drunks. I've even sustained a few kicks to the shins from misbehaving boys who don't respect the law."

Ivy's tumultuous emotions wouldn't allow her to speak. She'd been correct. He wanted to extend a well-mannered apology. Nothing more. Exhausted, she swayed on her feet and slumped onto the bench.

"Are you all right?" His concern sounded sincere.

"Just finish what you came here to say. My head is pounding. I need to go home and sleep."

Ernest pulled the ring out of his pocket and reached for her hand. "There's only one thing I need to say, Ivy. Will you marry me? Please?"

Ivy gasped and stared at her hand as he slipped the exquisite ring back onto her finger. "Ernest, I don't know…"

"Say yes. Please. I acted like a complete fool, letting my ego run amok. Letting my pride come between us. I realize you had no choice but to distance yourself from the likes of Charlie Connors and your brothers." Ernest lifted her hand to his lips. "Please agree to be my wife. I'll never question anything you do again. Ever."

Ivy burst into tears. "You still want to marry me?" she blubbered.

"More than anything."

Ivy threw herself into his arms. "Yes. Oh, yes. A hundred times yes. I love you so much."

Ernest's lips found hers and she returned his kiss with an intensity she didn't know she possessed. How was it possible to love someone so thoroughly that you'd give your life for theirs?

Ivy broke the kiss; she needed Ernest to understand. "I'll never lie to you again. You can trust me. I'll be the kind of wife you deserve: honest, responsible, loving. I promise to make you proud..."

Ernest gently placed a finger on her lips. "Stop it. I know who you are, and why I fell in love with you."

Ivy's eyes welled with tears. Her prayers had been answered. He'd forgiven her.

Ernest reached for her hands. "I hope my future wife remains on the right side of the law. I doubt my handcuffs will fit such dainty wrists."

Ivy laughed. "I promise you, never will you have the need to test them for size."

"I'm happy to hear it." Ernest stood and guided Ivy to her feet. "So, how about an autumn wedding. Would that suit?"

"Autumn is my favorite time of year. Late September would be perfect." Her exhaustion forgotten, Ivy started up the path, pulling Ernest along with her. "Come on. I can't wait to tell Aunt Minnie our wonderful news."

CHAPTER 20

Chicago
Thursday, June 9, 1892

Blake checked into his well-appointed room at the Great Northern Hotel. He dug the whiskey bottle out of the bottom of his suitcase and poured himself a shot. He took a deep breath and downed the liquid comfort in one gulp. He slumped onto the canopied bed as everything that had happened in Spirit Creek replayed in his head.

He wanted nothing more than to crawl between the clean white sheets and sleep for a week. But he'd been ordered to meet with his boss at Pinkerton headquarters in a half hour. Feeling the effects in his bones of every long, bumpy mile that he'd travelled between Spirit Creek and Pinkerton headquarters, he dragged himself off the bed, locked up his room, and headed out to his meeting.

"Connors!" called his colleague as Blake entered the Pinkerton office building on Washington Street.

"Barnes," acknowledged Blake, shaking his fellow agent's hand. "How are you doing? I haven't seen you in months."

"I'm well. And you?"

"No complaints. Still on the right side of the grass as they say." Blake hid his fatigue, happy to be seeing a familiar face. A person he knew he could trust unequivocally. "Just here to report on my latest case."

"Well, I'll leave you to it then." The man started down the hallway and then turned back for a brief moment. "Hell of thing about Burton."

Burton? What about the fellow? Had Burton shown up here after disappearing so suddenly during the shootout outside Spirit Creek?

Noticing his colleague had disappeared from the hallway, Blake continued toward his boss's office. He straightened his apparel, removed his Stetson, and knocked on the door.

"Come in!" bellowed the familiar male voice.

Blake opened the door and poked his head inside. "Connors here as ordered."

"Come in and take a seat." Christopher Sullivan waved Blake toward a chair.

"Thank you, sir. Here's a full written report on my assignment in Spirit Creek." Blake settled into the stuffed leather chair across from his superior and handed him the hand-written pages. "We arrested both gangs as we'd hoped. Didn't anticipate Walter Bailey being killed during the arrests, and we expected a different outcome with the Connors gang."

"Please forgive my tone and impatience earlier. Shouldn't take disturbing news out on my men," apologized his boss while he perused the written report.

"Disturbing news?" ventured Blake. Surely his boss wasn't about to reprimand him for the bank robbers' deaths. None of it could have been prevented. Leastwise, not in his opinion anyway. Unforeseen things happened on occasion, and there was no fair way to assign blame for such occurrences.

"One of our men in the field was murdered. Samuel Burton. Good, reliable agent. Family man with a wife and three sons." The man met Blake's eyes. "Damn shame."

"I met Burton in Spirit Creek. Helped with the jail break and pursuit of the escaped prisoners," offered Blake.

Mr. Sullivan stared at him for a long moment. "What in blazes are you talking about?"

"Burton. You sent him to Spirit Creek to help with…"

"Samuel Burton was murdered in Butte, Montana almost a month ago. He was never dispatched to Spirit Creek." His boss chewed on the end of his cigar, knocking a few ashes off the lit end.

Blake swallowed hard. His suspicions were being proven correct. "What did Burton look like? Tall, brown hair…"

His boss was shaking his head already. "Short, stocky, red hair and blue eyes."

"Hell. That means some bastard impersonated Samuel Burton while I was in Spirit Creek. Showed up a few hours after my pa and brother's arrest. Shortly after my family members discovered who I worked for and that, in their minds, I'd double-crossed them."

"Who was this fellow do you suppose?" blurted Mr. Sullivan.

"I haven't a clue. But my gut told me there was something a little off about the fellow. Just showed up without me being informed. And then the man disappeared after the shootout with my family and the people who broke them out of their cell. As you'll read in my report, someone blew out the side of the jailhouse with dynamite."

"Dynamite!" Christopher Sullivan leapt out of his chair and paced the office floor, cigar hanging out of the side of his mouth. "This business is becoming stranger by the minute. I'd bet a year's wages the fellow you're talking about killed Burton and took over his identity."

"I believe he had Burton's badge with him," confirmed Blake. "Now that I think about it, one of the local lawmen mentioned that during the shootout it appeared most of the bullets were being directed at me. A bullet grazed one of my shoulders."

"You were shot!" bellowed his boss.

"It's all in the report." Blake waved off his boss's concern. "Just a scratch. Nothing serious. The local sawbones fixed me up."

"Glad to hear that."

"The fellow impersonating Burton showed up shortly after the robbery. Do you suppose my cover had been blown already? Had he been hired a while ago to kill me? Perhaps by some other gang who I'd had a hand in arresting? Or maybe someone I arrested figured out I wasn't who he thought I was?"

"Seems possible." His boss scratched his chin. "Well, your undercover career is over, Connors. We'll need to assign you to regular cases from now on. Sending you out undercover again would be suicide."

"I agree, but I've been contemplating another option." He'd heard stories about fellow agents' recent deadly involvement in strikebreaking measures, and he questioned whether to continue his employ with an agency earning itself a negative reputation of late. With the Pinkerton name suffering, and his feelings for Gertie growing each day, he'd thought long and hard about his future. He felt certain in time the Pinkerton name would regain any lost respect, but did he really want to continue this path in life?

"We could probably find you a position here in the office if you…"

"Actually, I've been giving serious thought to retiring," admitted Blake.

Mr. Sullivan stood open-mouthed and speechless.

CHAPTER 21

Spirit Creek
Saturday, September 24, 1892

Ivy's hands skimmed the bodice of the sky-blue silk wedding dress as she admired herself in the cheval mirror in her aunt's hotel room. The widowed owner of the Spirit Creek Clothing Emporium designed and sewed the gown especially for her.

"My word, Dottie, you outdid yourself with this gorgeous creation. It's the most beautiful thing I've ever seen," exclaimed Ivy, twirling in a circle and enjoying the movement of the voluminous skirts.

"The gown is marvelous," agreed Aunt Minnie, discreetly drying her tears. "And you deserve it, my dear."

Ivy turned and met her aunt's eyes. "Thank you so much for paying Dottie's bill. I can't imagine what this must have cost you."

Aunt Minnie waved away her niece's concern. "Don't give it a second thought. I'm delighted to do it. You know you're like a daughter to me. I never would have imagined we'd find a shop offering custom-made gowns right here in Spirit Creek."

"The town is growing in size every week it seems." Ivy gave a somewhat tearful Dottie a warm hug, feeling her own eyes well with unshed tears. "Thank you so much. It's exactly what I envisioned when we talked."

Dottie waved her hands in front of her face. "Enough tears. I'll be bawling like a newborn if you don't stop it."

Ivy turned her attention to Aunt Minnie. "I can't tell you how pleased I am that you decided to stay all summer so you could be here for my wedding."

"Darling, I haven't one reason to rush home with only an old boarding house my employees are capable of running without me and a handful of friends waiting there. Besides, I couldn't miss your wedding."

Dottie gently elbowed Ivy in the ribs. "Don't let her fool you. Since she's caught Reverend Gerald's eye, she may never return home. I could be making another wedding dress before the year is over."

Aunt Minnie gasped and her face turned crimson. "The reverend and I…we're only friends," she blurted.

Ivy burst into laughter.

Dottie shook her head. "Not the way he gazes at you when you're not looking. All dreamy-eyed and love struck."

"Dottie Hartley, a man of God does not walk around looking love struck," protested Aunt Minnie.

"Our reverend does," agreed Ivy. "And I hope you remain open to the possibility of something starting up between you. When he asks if he might court you, please say yes."

The spinster threw up her hands. "Oh, pooh. No man would want to court me, for heaven's sake."

"Aunt Minnie, Reverend Gerald seems close to your age if not a little older, and he's never married either. Maybe he's just been waiting for the right woman. For you," suggested Ivy, tenderly running her hands up and down her aunt's arms.

"I agree," said Dottie. "You make a wonderful couple. And the poor reverend has been alone all these years, serving the community. He deserves a little happiness."

Just then someone knocked on the door.

"Come in," called Ivy.

"I'm running late but I'm here now." Sadie Maxwell, the matron of honor, stepped inside. "Goodness, I haven't been this disorganized since I helped Maggie with the annual Carlyle Community Picnic last month." And then she spotted the bride in her dress. "Ivy, you look beautiful!"

"Thank you." Ivy smiled. "You look so nice in your gown, too."

Sadie gazed down at the pale blue satin gown that fit her perfectly and adjusted the lacy shawl draped over her shoulders. "I bought this gown when I attended that horrid finishing school. I've never worn it because it was always a little large, and I never got around to having it altered. Now, I'm just delighted that it fits me perfectly after giving birth to Abigail."

Aunt Minnie crossed the floor and extracted a small velvet box from her jewelry case hidden in the top dresser drawer. "Ivy, these ear clips belonged to your grandmother, and I insist you wear them today. Something old. Your gown is both new and blue, and Dottie let you borrow that lovely feathered hairpiece. I would say you're set to be wed."

Ivy swiped at the tear that trickled down her cheek when her aunt opened the box and showed her the diamond earrings inside. "Thank you so much. I've admired those jewels on your ears several Sundays since you arrived in town."

"When I pass from this world, they will go to you, my dear. Wear them in good health." Aunt Minnie handed the box to Ivy.

"Let me help you put them on." Sadie clipped the diamonds onto Ivy's ears and then took a step back. "Lovely, but not as beautiful as you."

"Thank you." Ivy hugged her friend.

"I spotted your groom and his brother standing outside the general store when I rode by in the carriage. Those two handsome devils are all spiffed up for the ceremony," teased Sadie.

Ivy commented, "Gertie told me, at every opportunity all week Donald has been annoying his brother about being the 'best man' and yet Ernest gets the bride."

"Ladies, please allow me a few minutes alone with my niece before we travel to the church," requested Aunt Minnie, brushing a piece of lint off of her navy satin gown, a recent custom purchase courtesy of Dottie.

"Of course, we'll head over there and you two come along when you're ready," said Sadie, accompanying the town's favorite seamstress out of the room.

Aunt Minnie reached for Ivy's hand. "What's troubling you? I can see in your eyes that your mind is preoccupied with something other than your wedding day."

"I'm just feeling a little guilty is all," confessed Ivy. "All of my dreams are coming true today. And yet, I never mourned my father's or Albert's deaths. Isn't that sinful?"

Ivy had tossed and turned in bed well into the wee hours last night. Her mind wouldn't settle. She imagined what her wedding day would be like. Wondered how she'd feel walking toward her handsome groom waiting for her at the altar. And then she reviewed all the arrangements a dozen times in her head, convinced she and Aunt Minnie had forgotten something. She still wasn't certain they hadn't.

Around two o'clock, she contemplated her father's and brother's deaths. She still had no inclination to mourn them. When her mother passed she'd cried herself to sleep for months. Cursed a God who would take her mother from her at such a young age, just when she herself was becoming a woman and needed her most. She hadn't returned to church until she attended Normal School and befriended a minister's daughter who'd help her put the loss of her mother into perspective.

Everyone grieves in their own way. Her friend's words popped into her head. What about not grieving at all? What if you could care less if your despicable father and brother lived or died? Had the heartless twosome's deplorable behavior toward her killed any affection she'd ever felt toward them?

After her ma's death, her pa had forbidden her to cry or show any sign of grieving. Instead, he demanded his meals be served on time and the house be cleaned. Pa even sent a note with her enabling her to purchase him a bottle of liquor from one of the saloons. She shivered remembering the voices of the drunken brutes in the establishment, whistling and leering at her, making advances toward her with lewd statements. She'd returned home safely with the bottle of liquor for the father she now hated, escorted by one of the owner's 'girls'. She'd heard the girl relaying a message from the owner to her father, offering him the opportunity to permit Ivy to work for him. That had been the last straw. She packed her meager belongings, disguised herself as a boy, and left shortly past midnight after her pa had passed out. She'd never looked back.

"Not at all. Those despicable men don't deserve a moment of grieving. Your father was a terrible parent, dragging his children into his life of crime. Don't waste a minute second-guessing yourself. You owe them nothing. You were wise to escape from them when you did." Aunt Minnie patted her hand.

"I just wish Blake could have been here. The man in the family. Someone to walk me down the aisle." Ivy sighed. That was the real reason for her melancholy. Mr. Waverly had volunteered to do the honors. Apparently, he'd been enlisted to act as father-of-the-bride on a few occasions. But he wasn't kin. He wasn't the brother she found herself loving again.

"Ronald will do the honors. He and Elizabeth are two of my favorite people in Spirit Creek. Such nice folks." Aunt Minnie donned her small navy hat and wrapped a lace shawl around her shoulders.

"Are you ready?" whispered Ivy. Her hands shook slightly, but she felt herself beaming. She'd convinced herself that, although she hadn't grieved for her kin, she was worthy of Ernest. Once she'd realized she deserved the man she loved so dearly, she'd drifted off into a deep sleep and had awoken surprisingly rested.

"Anytime you are, my dear." Aunt Minnie hugged her tightly. "I cannot find the words to tell you how proud I am of you."

"Thank you. I love you so much, Auntie. Nothing could spoil this day."

Just then, a loud knock on the door startled them.

* * *

Blake stood in the Spirit Creek Hotel's second-floor hallway, shifting from one foot to the other. He couldn't have wiped the smile off his face if he'd tried.

"Does she know you're here?" asked Donald Jones.

"Not at all. Wanted it to be a surprise."

"Oh, she'll be surprised. Be prepared to catch her when she faints," warned Donald.

Just then the door opened and Ivy stood before him, staring in disbelief. His breath caught. His little sister looked so grown up, standing there in her wedding dress. For a moment he was equally speechless.

"You're not seeing things, sis." Blake grinned when his sister's mouth moved but no sound came out. "I figured you'd need someone to walk you down the aisle today."

"You...you…you came for my wedding?" she stammered in amazement.

"Wouldn't miss it."

Ivy grabbed her brother's hand and dragged him into the room. "You're looking at the happiest bride in the entire state of Montana."

Donald cleared his throat. "I'll mosey on over to the church and check up on my brother."

Aunt Minnie hugged Blake. "I'm so thankful you travelled here for Ivy's big day."

"I can't believe you're here." Ivy beamed from ear to ear and Blake knew he'd made the right decision.

All the hours he'd spent poring over Pinkerton Agency files and mug shots looking for the fellow who'd impersonated Burton was worth seeing the smile on his little sister's face. And he'd found the man. Herbert Wallens. Blake now remembered arresting him years ago, and he learned that Herbert had been released from prison recently and no doubt held a grudge.

Blake smiled at his sister. "I needed to be here to tell you that no one should live life on another person's terms. Forget who your father was and what he did. Just look to the rosy future ahead of you. Ernest loves you so much. I couldn't have asked for a better husband for you."

"You're going to have my eyes all red and puffy for my wedding," sniffed Ivy, dabbing at her eyes. "Ernest even hired that newspaper photograph man, Arthur MacDonald, owner of the *Spirit Creek Chronicle*."

"Then I had better not tell you the rest of it," warned Blake, grinning.

Ivy reached for the handkerchief Aunt Minnie handed her. "It won't matter now."

"Your news will keep, Blake. We need to head over to the church or the bride will be more than fashionably late," warned Aunt Minnie. "Have you got everything, Ivy?"

"Yes, let's go. I don't want Ernest thinking I've changed my mind." Ivy clasped her hands together, beaming at her brother. "I still can't believe it. If I'm dreaming, please don't wake me until after the ceremony."

Blake wrapped her hand around his arm. "You're not dreaming. And you're about to become Mrs. Ernest Jones."

"Oh, I love the sound of that. Let's hurry." Ivy hugged her brother's arm before he led her out of the hotel and walked her to the church.

* * *

Ernest tugged on his shirt collar.

"Won't be long now," whispered Reverend Gerald, standing beside the groom in front of the congregation.

Ernest smiled weakly. The church walls seemed to close in on him, inch by inch. The humid and suffocating air felt like what he imagined a steam bath would, having only read about them but never experiencing one. He dug his handkerchief out of his pocket and wiped his brow. Funny, no one else seemed to be sweating. Dang it. Waiting for Ivy to enter the church might kill him. She wouldn't have changed her mind. Would she?

Just running a little late claimed Donald when he arrived a few minutes ago. Blake had surprised her, and the shock of seeing her brother at her door would be cause alone for her tardiness. At least, he hoped that was the sole reason for her delay.

He shifted his weight to his other foot and blew out his breath. As long as he didn't look up at all those people occupying the pews, he'd be all right. Dang it, he hated being the center of attention. But he'd do it today, for Ivy's sake. After all, this would be her only wedding day if he had any say in the matter. He wanted it to be perfect for her.

Ernest glanced over at his best man standing beside him, a mirror image to himself, dressed in a new suit, crisp white shirt and polished boots. Born fifteen months apart, the two of them could almost pass for twins. Best man indeed. He'd endured Donald's ribbing for days now, but he sincerely hoped that someday his younger brother would find a woman he loved as much as Ernest loved Ivy.

Donald whispered, "You look like you're either about to faint or make a run for it."

Ernest chuckled aloud and glanced at the smiling reverend. Donald looked prepared to chase him down if he high-tailed it out the door. Ernest knew he appeared nervous. He was. But not about marrying Ivy.

Speaking of Ivy, where on earth was she?

If Ernest was honest with himself, perhaps he was a little nervous about the whole shebang. Shouldn't the bride be nervous, not the groom? Or was that afterward as the wedding night loomed?

Ernest grimaced, recalling his father's speech last Thursday evening concerning his marital duties as a husband. Having waited for his wedding night to experience first-time lovemaking with his bride, he hadn't any idea so much went into satisfying a wife. Although he feared his face turned several shades of red during the conversation with his pa, he was ready to pleasure Ivy in every way. Discussing it all with his pa had been a little disturbing, but it helped to explain why his pa had fathered a dozen children.

Next, Ernest recalled everything the Pinkerton agent had shared with him and Donald last night. Holy smokes, and he'd thought the bank robbery matter was behind them. He still couldn't wrap his mind around all the warnings Blake had given him and Donald after they finished moving all of Ernest's belongings into the new house he'd built for his bride.

Of course, Ernest's father and brothers and friends had helped with the building to ensure the project was completed in time. Now, the home was finished and ready for them. He'd built or purchased only the bare necessities knowing that Ivy would want to furnish their home herself, and pick out all the feminine fripperies that women liked. He'd refused to move into the home until his bride could join him there. Tonight was the night!

After they helped Ernest move into his house, Donald suggested Blake share the cabin with him while he visited Spirit Creek. Blake thanked Ernest's brother for his thoughtfulness and readily agreed to the arrangement. And Blake would be close at hand to help capture the outlaw, Herbert Wallens.

Every lawman he knew including Bob Sanders believed Wallens would attempt another try at killing Blake who'd be living his life looking over his shoulder until Wallens was arrested or killed. Either way suited Ernest, since more than four murders could be attributed to the outlaw who'd only recently been released from prison and already had killed again. And a Pinkerton detective no less.

Ernest startled from his musings when he heard the first chords on the piano, and then Ivy walked into the church. Her beautiful gown shimmered in the candlelight, her radiant smile lit up the room. She looked like an angel. The groom lost his heart to her, all over again.

* * *

Ivy gasped as she entered the church on her brother's arm.

True to tradition, the community ladies had decorated the church beautifully. Several arrangements of autumn flowers in gold and rust and red hues sat in front of a large arch covered in autumn leaves. One large bouquet covered half the top of the church piano. Evergreen sprigs and contrasting colorful fall blooms were bound together with red ribbons and tied to the ends of every pew. A lit taper occupied each windowsill and provided a mesmerizing glow.

Appearing decidedly with child, Ellie Rutherford, the lawyer's wife who inherited Sarah Grayson's beautiful gardens when her husband bought the widow's home, handed Ivy a bridal bouquet of purple asters and deep pink chrysanthemums. Several sprigs of needlepoint ivy, so fitting for this particular bride, peeked out from among the blooms tied together with a wide white ribbon. "I created this especially for you," she whispered.

Ivy gasped, "Sadie told me you were making me a bouquet, but I had no idea. It's wonderful, Ellie. Thank you so much."

"Your dress is lovely. You're a beautiful bride." Ellie kissed Ivy's cheek.

"Thank you," whispered Ivy, holding her emotions in check. She'd promised herself she wouldn't cry in the church and spoil her appearance for the photograph.

"Are you ready?" whispered Blake, patting her hand.

Ivy nodded, not trusting herself to speak. She clasped her brother's arm a little tighter.

As they started down the aisle, Ivy gazed ahead and met Ernest's eyes. The groom stood beside Reverend Gerald, visibly shaking. Ivy smiled at him. Her brave lawman could look down the barrel of an outlaw's gun, but he appeared to be panicking at the thought of saying 'I do'.

Blake took a step back after seeing her down the aisle and leaving her at Ernest's side.

"Are you all right?" whispered Ivy.

Ernest smiled weakly.

Reverend Gerald cleared his throat. "Dearly beloved, we are gathered together…"

Ivy looked deep into Ernest's eyes and blocked out every sound, including the reverend's words. How was it possible to love this man so much? She couldn't believe how happy he made her, when he wasn't driving her crazy, of course. She stifled the laugh that almost escaped her lips.

Two days ago, he'd given her a male kitten, completely black with four white paws. Someone to keep her company when he worked at night, he'd said. The critter had been running wild in the schoolhouse, tearing up pieces of paper, and playing in her mending basket, having a wonderful time. She'd been threatening to name him Trouble. Aunt Minnie insisted on Boots. Ivy had to admit the cute little fellow had stolen her heart. If she could only teach him to leave her yarn alone.

"Ivy Connors, do you take this man…"

She certainly would, for the rest of her time on this earth. No one could complete her life like Ernest. She wanted him, needed him, forever.

"You bet, I do," she answered at the appropriate time, amid a smattering of chuckles from the congregation.

CHAPTER 22

"You may kiss your bride, Ernest," announced Reverend Gerald.

Ernest placed his hands on Ivy's cheeks and gently kissed her warm and welcoming lips. Ivy's hands rested on his upper arms while she returned the kiss, blushing profusely.

The newlyweds broke apart and Reverend Gerald announced, "For the first time, may I present to you Mr. and Mrs. Ernest Jones."

Ernest and Ivy turned and walked hand-in-hand down the aisle amid applause and shouts of congratulations. They stepped outside, standing on the front step while waiting for the best man and maid of honor to join them.

"Arthur MacDonald set up his camera in the churchyard and he'll be taking our wedding picture shortly." Ernest whispered the reminder in Ivy's ear and kissed her cheek. "I love you."

"I love you, too."

Just as Blake and Aunt Minnie stepped outside behind Donald and Sadie, two shots rang out.

"Get back inside!" yelled Ernest and Blake in unison.

Blake dragged his aunt backward while Ernest and Donald hurried inside with Ivy and Sadie in tow.

"Someone is firing a gun!" exclaimed Sadie, incredulously. "Is that in celebration? Or is someone drunk?"

"Neither, I suspect." Ernest turned toward the ladies. "Stay in here until we tell you it's safe to come out. Make sure no one else leaves either."

The three women nodded their heads and reached for each other's hands.

Ernest, Donald and Blake exchanged looks and then tentatively stepped through the doorway.

"I heard two shots," observed Ernest. "A pistol and a rifle."

Another round of shots rang out.

"Me too," confirmed Blake, ducking back inside the church with Ernest on his heels.

"Wallens?" questioned Blake.

"Not a doubt in my mind. But who else is shooting at us? Did he bring someone with him?" speculated Ernest.

"Or is it somebody else holding a grudge? How many bank robbers you put away?" inquired Donald.

"Dozens," muttered Blake.

Ernest reached for his gun and came up empty-handed. "Dammit, I'm unarmed."

"Same here," grumbled Donald, standing at his brother's side.

Blake shook his head. "Didn't seem right, being in church and all."

"I guess we'll have to rely on the others," stated Ernest.

"Others!" exclaimed Donald. "What others?"

Ernest shrugged. "I deputized Luke Carlyle and Robert Morgan this morning. On a hunch. Figured better safe than…"

"So Luke and Robert are out there somewhere," reiterated Blake.

"Stationed them out of sight in their own carriages across the street, one on each side of the front of the church."

"Ernest Jones, aren't you the crafty one." Blake slapped his fellow lawman on the back. "I'm impressed."

"Learned from the best. Let's hope those ranchers figured out where that shooting came from. Haven't heard any gunshots lately. Maybe they've already arrested Wallens and whoever else is out there," suggested Donald.

One at a time, the three lawmen stuck their heads outside and ventured onto the top step. "See anything?" asked Blake.

"Nervous horses hitched to those rigs. The horses tied to the hitching post are dancing and tugging on the reins. Nothing else," offered Ernest.

"I got one of them," called Robert Morgan from across the street. "Tried to sneak up and shoot me in the back. Got him first."

"Good," replied Ernest. "Where's the other varmint?"

A raggedly-dressed man stepped out from the corner of the church. "Blake Connors, you yeller-bellied coward. Step out here, face me like a man."

"Not damn likely, Wallens, knowing you'll shoot me in cold blood." Blake remained standing to the side, his body partly concealed by the other lawmen.

"Then I'll kill the whole damn lot of you!" shouted the outlaw, raising his pistol and taking aim.

A shot rang out from behind the clump of bushes nearest the graveyard.

Wallens's expression changed from rage to shock. "What…" The outlaw fell backward, and his body landed face up on the ground. Unseeing eyes looked to the sky, and a bright red stain spread across the front of his grimy white shirt.

"No doubt he's dead." Ernest moved off the steps and walked toward the corpse.

"Another wasted life. Like my father and my brother."

Donald slapped Blake on the back. "A man makes his own choices in life. Not up to others to change that. And they probably couldn't if they'd tried."

"You're right." Blake stood over the body.

Luke Carlyle and Robert Morgan stepped forward, rifles pointed toward the ground. The town's temporary deputies joined the others looking down on the deceased. "Is he the fellow you warned us about, Ernest?"

"That's him all right," confirmed Blake. "What about the other one?"

"Take a look see," said Robert, heading back across the street.

The trio of lawmen followed Robert and Luke. Boots crunched across the blanket of dead leaves as they stepped behind a group of cottonwoods where a man lay dead atop a heap of fallen autumn foliage. The outlaw's rifle lay across his chest, and even in death, his finger remained hooked around the weapon's trigger.

Blake hunkered down, checked for a pulse. "Ike Pemberton. Walter Bailey's half-brother. Ike rode with Jesse James for a spell, if I remember correctly. Might be wrong about that though. Not certain. Guess Ike took it into his head to avenge Walter's killing."

"Thanks for saving our hides." Ernest shook the ranchers' hands. "I'm glad that you fellows agreed to be deputized and remain out here instead of attending the ceremony."

Luke nodded. "Couldn't have all the local lawmen unarmed and the town unprotected. Must admit I was little shocked when I realized two of them were shooting at you fellows."

"Thought I was seeing things," added Robert.

"Well, your quick thinking and good reflexes saved our lives," offered Donald.

"Glad you didn't hesitate to use those rifles." Ernest stood hands on hips, "I'll send Sheriff Sanders a telegraph to let him know what happened."

"I'll send a telegraph to Pinkerton headquarters also," said Blake. "Hopefully, this message makes it through. Apparently, the one I sent about Burton when he disappeared after the shootout was misplaced. My boss never received it anyway."

"Well, you boys would have done the same for us." Luke stuck his rifle under the driver's bench of his carriage.

"You a married man now, Ernest?" Robert hid his own rifle out of sight under his carriage's seat.

"Yep."

"Congratulations," said Luke and Robert in unison.

Just then the undertaker pulled up in his rickety wooden wagon. "Ernest warned me there could be some shooting today. I headed over here when I heard the gunshots. It's been a busy day, unfortunately."

"What do you mean?" ventured Blake.

"Doc sent a fellow over this morning to fetch me."

"Why?" exclaimed Ernest. "Nobody told me about any ruckus or killing last night in any of the saloons."

"Mayor Barker's wife died in childbirth last night. Both her and baby, gone." The fellow shook his head. "Damn shame. And now Barker is left with five little girls to raise alone."

"Oh, man. That's too bad." Blake dragged his hand down his face, sending a prayer of thanks heavenward that the bullet he'd taken hadn't been closer to his heart. He could have been riding in this wagon himself a while ago.

"Hell of a job, this," muttered the undertaker. "Especially days like today. Give me a hand, boys."

The men helped load the dead bodies.

"They being buried here? Or you sending them somewhere else, Ernest?"

Blake pointed out each fellow in turn. "Far as I know, Ike Pemberton's only living relative was Walter Bailey and I doubt Walter's widow cares where we bury her brother-in-law. As I recall from the Pinkerton records, Herbert Wallens has a sister living in Butte. She married a fellow who operates a general store there. Law-abiding, hard-working folks. Doubt they care one whit about her outlaw brother's final resting place either. Just stuff each of them in a simple pine box and bury them in the farthest corner of your graveyard."

"Got it. Pine boxes. Wooden markers." The undertaker leapt onto the buggy's seat and waved toward the church before grabbing the reins. "Sorry to disturb the day's celebrations, Ernest. I'll get this rig out of here right away before the decent folks come out of the church."

"Thanks. I appreciate that." Ernest sent the fellow off with a salute.

"Guess that puts an end to our worries," observed Donald. "Let's get on with the celebrations."

Blake touched Ernest's sleeve and briefly met eyes with the other men. "I suppose it's too much to expect folks to not wonder where the mayor is when he doesn't put in an appearance at the wedding. Or for nobody to mention what happened to his wife. But I sure hate spoiling the day for Ivy with such sad news."

Luke rested his hand on Blake's shoulder. "We won't say anything though, unless someone else mentions it first."

They all nodded in agreement.

Ernest strode across the churchyard and raced up the steps. He threw open the church's double doors. "It's safe to come out now, folks. More importantly, where is my beautiful bride?"

The newlyweds received hugs and handshakes and congratulations. Ernest was cheered for his wise forethought in deputizing Luke and Robert who'd told their wives that they had to miss the ceremony because a scuffle had broken out in one of the saloons. Maggie and Hattie forgave them their little white lies. It appeared a lot of folks saw the benefit to the occasional little white lie, if offered for a purpose and doing no one any real harm.

While the wedding guests mingled in groups outside the church, Arthur MacDonald, despite a slightly shaking hand, managed to take the wedding picture of the bride and groom and another one with their attendants standing in front of a grouping of trees displaying a beautiful array of autumn colors.

Soon, everyone headed to the hotel for a luncheon and to continue the festivities.

* * *

Ivy waved to Reverend Gerald, standing on the front steps of the church. "See you at the hotel," she called. He waved back.

Ernest helped her into the one-horse buggy he'd rented for the occasion. Suspecting the limited means of a small-town sheriff, Ivy appreciated the thoughtfulness of the unnecessary expense. The groom soon wrestled her dress's voluminous skirts under control, and Ivy tucked them into place alongside her.

Ernest leapt up beside her on the bench seat. "All ready?"

"Yes. But tell me, Ernest, what the devil happened out here?" demanded Ivy.

"Sweetheart, there are more pleasant things to discuss."

"Ernest Jones. Do not brush off my question." Ivy grasped his arm. "Tell me what happened. Did one of those men attempt to kill my brother?"

Ernest met her eyes.

Ivy saw his hesitation and assumed she would need to provide further encouragement for him to share the incident with her. Her new husband was considerate of womenfolk to a fault. Just as she was about to protest his reluctance, he sighed loudly.

"There were two of them…"

"Two!" blurted Ivy, feeling herself pale.

Ernest slammed his jaws shut.

Ivy touched his arm. "Tell me. I peeked outside and almost fainted when I spotted the undertaker's wagon parked beside the churchyard gate."

"You weren't supposed to glimpse that." Reluctantly, he shared the tale of the attempted ambush on Robert, and divulged the details of Luke having no choice but to shoot the second fellow as well when he threatened the three lawmen on the church steps.

"So both of them came looking for my brother, intent on murdering him?"

"Appears that way. Fortunately, I suspected as much and had two deputies waiting for them. Luke and Robert definitely saved our hides." Ernest shook his head. "If the possibility of trouble hadn't been niggling at my mind, I don't want to even consider what could have been the outcome."

"Who were they?"

"Walter Bailey's brother-in-law, out to avenge his killing during the robbery. Blake arrested the other fellow years ago. The newly-released prisoner was looking for revenge."

"Is this ever going to stop?" whispered Ivy. "Blake is never going to find peace, is he?"

Ernest patted her hand. "I don't know, sweetheart. I hope someday these fellows will allow him to get on with his life and put bygones behind them."

"Some men don't ever forgive a betrayal." Ivy met his eyes. "My father wouldn't. If anyone wronged him in his eyes, there would be heck to pay."

She noticed Ernest smiling at her version of the expression but cussing wasn't in her nature. No doubt, her ladylike language and behavior had attracted the good Christian gentleman to her in the first place. For a second, she just gazed at him. Her husband. At times lately, she'd lost hope that this day would ever come. But here he was, seated beside her. Hers forever.

"Troubles us lawmen something fierce, whenever there's heck to pay," he mumbled, smiling broadly.

"Don't say another word," she scolded him for teasing her. "Pa would travel to the ends of the world for payback. These other outlaws must be of a similar mind."

"You could be right, but I'm hoping Blake finds a way to distance himself from them eventually," offered Ernest.

"Oh, he must. I couldn't bear it if something happened to him, now that we've finally found our way back into each other's lives."

"Well, you know I'll do everything possible to assure that he stays safe."

"As long as he's here in Spirit Creek, I know folks will be keeping watch. I'll worry when Blake leaves town though. Meantime, we have a wedding to celebrate, Mr. Jones." Ivy hugged his arm as he reined the horses up to the sidewalk beside the hotel.

"We most certainly do, Mrs. Jones. Don't give this business with your brother another thought today. Let's just concentrate on us." Ernest helped her down from the seat. "Have I mentioned how lovely you look?"

Ivy shook out her skirts and hooked her hand around her husband's arm. She gazed into his eyes, smiling. "Thank you. You couldn't look more handsome. Now, please lead the way."

Ernest guided her up the hotel's wide steps, ensuring she didn't trip on her billowing skirts. She felt like a princess in her dress and she intended to fully enjoy the remainder of her special day. But she couldn't help worrying about her brother's future with the Pinkerton Agency. Now that she'd been reunited with her favorite sibling, she refused to lose him again. If only she knew of a way to ensure his safety?

CHAPTER 23

Ivy almost swooned when she stepped into the Spirit Creek Hotel's ballroom. The entire room was decorated with white streamers, white paper bells, and colorful autumn flowers. Fresh evergreen sprigs tied around lit candles served as centerpieces atop round tables covered in white linen cloths. The scent of pine permeated every corner of the room. The tables were set with sparkling crystal glassware, red rose-patterned bone china, and white cloth napkins, including the rectangular head table up front for the bride and groom and their attendants. The most tempting aromas wafted from the kitchen and made her mouth water in anticipation of her wedding meal.

Aunt Minnie strode across the ballroom floor toward Ivy and her niece's new husband.

Ivy hugged her aunt tightly. "I can't believe you planned this elaborate party for Ernest and me. Thank you so much."

"You're more than welcome, sweetheart."

"But, Auntie, this must be costing you a fortune," whispered Ivy.

Aunt Minnie waved away her concern. "What else will I spend my money on?"

"But..."

"Not another word. I've done quite nicely running the boarding house after your grandparents passed away. I cannot think of a better purpose for spending some of my savings."

At the mention of her grandparents, Ivy's fingers touched her grandmother's sparkling earrings that she wore. She could only recall meeting her grandmother on two occasions, each time for Christmas dinner when she was quite young. Granny had smelled like roses, a strong heady scent that had bothered her nose and caused a series of sneezes. She smiled, recalling a tight hug followed by a pat on the head and a gift of a lacy handkerchief. Her mother later explained the gift had been hand-embroidered by her granny. Ivy still had the handkerchief tucked into a box of knickknacks and favorite things. She would pass it down to her own daughter some day.

Ivy pulled herself from her musings. She knew it would prove useless to argue with her aunt once she'd made up her mind about something. And it was too late to prevent her plans now anyway. "Thank you again, Auntie."

"Just enjoy yourself," encouraged her aunt.

Reverend Gerald appeared at their side, resplendent in his dark suit and clerical collar. "What a wonderful celebration you've planned for your niece, Miss Patterson."

"Thank you, and I insist you call me Minnie." Her aunt actually blushed and fiddled with her ear. "Would you consider sitting with me during the wedding meal, Reverend?"

The preacher smiled. "I'd be honored to dine with you, Minnie. And you must call me Lionel."

Ivy now considered Dottie's accusations about her aunt and the reverend more than gossip. She couldn't recall ever hearing Reverend Gerald's first name before. *Lionel.* Well, who knew?

"Lionel, we'll sit at that table up front near Ernest's family." Her aunt beamed. "And could I please ask that you say a blessing before we eat?"

The reverend nodded. "I consider it a must."

Minnie smiled. "I suppose it is. And I'm pleased you're here with us to do the honors."

Ivy wandered away, allowing her aunt and the reverend some privacy to continue to get to know each other. Perhaps she would acquire an uncle some day. She never considered the possibility that such a thought would cross her mind.

"How are you standing up with all the day's excitement, sweetheart?" Ernest slipped his arm around his bride's waist.

"Goodness, I can barely breathe," admitted Ivy. "With the

shootings outside the church. And this unexpected surprise. Aunt Minnie never ceases to amaze me. And now she's chatting up the reverend on a first name basis if you please."

Ernest gaped. "Reverend Gerald and your aunt?"

"The two of them are acting like a couple of teenagers at a harvest social." Ivy giggled. "*Uncle Lionel.* Has a nice ring to it, I think."

"Ivy, you're impossible." Ernest pulled her close and kissed her lips.

"Now. Now. Time enough for that later." Florence Jones playfully chastised the newly-weds with a twinkle in her eye. "Please take your seats at the front table. The ladies in the kitchen are ready to serve the meal."

Ivy pulled away from her husband. "Thank you, Mrs. Jones."

"Oh, pooh. No more Mrs. Jones. Please call me Mother. And I wouldn't say no to another grandchild," she hinted with a wink for Ivy.

Ivy felt her cheeks burning.

Ernest chuckled. "We'll see what we can do, Ma."

Florence clasped her son's hand. "You do that." And then she headed off toward another group of guests, encouraging them to take a seat.

Ivy sat beside Ernest seated on her left with Donald on the right. Blake sat on the other side of Donald. "All those hours of planning. I can't believe the day is almost over."

Blake peeked around Donald. "Not quite. Save a dance for your brother."

Ivy laughed. "Of course I will. Wasn't I the one who taught you to dance before your big date with Rebecca…what was her last name?"

"Dang if I remember." Blake gazed across the room.

Ivy noticed his attention centered on the pretty hotel maid, busily helping pass platters of food. She wore a large white apron over an emerald-green party dress. "I see Mrs. Davidson has Gertie helping in the kitchen tonight. She's dressed a little fancy for kitchen work."

"That she is, but she's finished at eight o'clock. And then she's coming to the dance as my guest." Blake's tone of voice suggested he'd issued his sister a challenge to argue with his plans.

"Sounds like a marvellous idea. You should spend as much time with Gertie as you can before your next assignment," declared Ivy.

"That won't be a problem at all. Now that that Wallens fellow will no longer be a problem, I've completed my final assignment with the Pinkerton Agency. As of an hour or so ago, I am no longer an agent, undercover or otherwise."

Ivy gasped. "You quit your job?"

"Retired, actually. My choice." Blake beamed.

"I…I don't believe it." Ivy leapt to her feet and hugged her brother's neck. "I won't have to worry about people shooting at you now."

"Well, not necessarily," suggested Ernest. "Yesterday early in the afternoon, Mayor Barker dropped by my house, heard Blake was back in town. When he learned that Blake would soon be retiring from the Pinkerton Agency, he offered him a job as the second town sheriff, right here in Spirit Creek. With the way the population keeps growing, we certainly need another sheriff. In fact, I'll be hiring a couple more deputies as well."

Blake shook Ernest's hand. "I'm officially retired now. You've got yourself a sheriff."

"Excellent. And you're settled in with Donald at the cabin. Welcome to town, Sheriff Connors," greeted Ernest.

"Thank you. I'm delighted to be working with good men like yourself and Donald."

"And I'm certain you'll be able to teach us a few new law-enforcement tricks. Spirit Creek is fortunate to have you," said Donald.

"Ernest, was this your idea?" asked Ivy.

"Nope. Barker mentioned it first, but I readily agreed with him. Donald and I certainly can use the help. Between dealing with cattle rustlers and bank robberies and Saturday night drunks, there's no end to the excitement around here," he suggested, grinning at Blake.

"Oh, there's a lot of exciting things that I find interesting in this town," mumbled Blake, glancing over at Gertie and winking at her.

"Blake, stop that. You'll get the girl fired." Ivy swatted her brother's arm and then returned to her seat beside Ernest.

"In that case, to make amends, I would just have to marry her," he hinted.

Ivy burst into laughter. "That solution wouldn't be a huge surprise to many folks."

"Me, an old married man with a beautiful wife. Hopefully, we'd have a few young ones later on." Blake shook his head. "Honest work.

Might be the end of the law-breaking Connors line and a start to a law-abiding, honest-living clan."

"Amen." Ivy clasped her new husband's arm and gazed into his eyes. "And I couldn't ask for a better man to spend the rest of my days with or more suitable father for my children."

"With a pa like Ernest and you for a mother, those children couldn't help but grow up to be law-biding, productive citizens like their parents," predicted Blake.

"And your young'uns would run wild like savages, I suppose?" teased his new co-worker.

"Hmm. Something about Gertie you're not telling me, Ernest?" Blake's eyebrows rose.

Ivy laughed.

Just then, she noticed Donald's face had paled.

"What's wrong, Donald?" Ivy gazed around the room, concerned her new brother-in-law had spotted another outlaw.

"*Who* is she?" he whispered, pointing toward the doorway.

Ivy laughed aloud. A beautiful, tall young woman wearing a deep pink gown, strawberry-blonde hair swept up and held in place with bejeweled combs, stood just inside the door. A pair of stunning, cornflower-blue eyes gazed around the room. When the young lady spotted Ivy, she smiled and waved. "Her name is Beth Anne McCarthy, and she's the new schoolteacher, here to replace me. She's been teaching for a month now, and I hear she's very good with the children. Plays the piano and the ukulele and sings with the children. They love her already by all accounts."

"She could sing me to sleep for the rest of my life." Donald stood, straightened his clothes and patted his hair. A broad smile creased his face. "I think it's time I met this new schoolteacher." He spoke to no one in particular, and then strode across the room intent on introducing himself to the town's newest citizen.

Ernest shook his head. "Good Lord, I think he's a goner already. If Donald marries her and Ronald Waverly has to hire yet another teacher, we'll never hear the end of it."

Aunt Minnie stepped up to the front of the table. "I heard what you were talking about a little while ago, and I cannot believe my sister and the likes of Charlie Connors produced such wonderful children as the two of you. I pray you'll all have many happy years together as family and friends."

"Did you hear the part about Blake becoming Spirit Creek's newest sheriff? He retired from the Pinkerton agency and he's settling down, probably marrying Gertie one of these days," predicted Ivy, winking at her brother.

"Land sakes," exclaimed Aunt Minnie, her hand flying to her chest. "Why I'm delighted to hear it. Especially since I've decided to settle here, too. I had tea with the folks who own the boarding house yesterday. They've been wanting to move to California, so I'm purchasing their business from them here and they're buying my boarding house from me. Imagine?"

"Aunt Minnie!" exclaimed Ivy and Blake in unison.

"Now, don't sound so shocked." Her aunt playfully swatted her nephew's sleeve. "I've discovered a number of reasons to move here now that there's nothing holding me back in California. This little town is the answer to my prayers. Family. Friends."

Ivy leapt out of her chair again and opened her arms. She added, "A man in your life. Perhaps something permanent in time. I'm so happy for you. I hope everything works out, exactly as you're hoping."

"Thank you, my dear." Her aunt moved into her niece's embrace and hugged her tightly. "Now I must return to my table. Be happy, my sweetheart."

"I couldn't be anything but happy with Ernest at my side." Ivy returned to her seat and sighed.

Whether family or friends or a virtual stranger, she'd never keep secrets from anyone ever again. No good would ever come of it, and ultimately, the secret would be revealed. She knew that now.

Knowing she'd be a mother someday, she wanted to be a good example for her children. Be the type of person her children could be proud to call their mother. Someone worthy of her children's love and respect, like Florence Jones. Someone worthy of a reverend's affections, like her Aunt Minnie. She intended to be the type of woman her husband could be proud to call his wife, her brother could be proud to call his sister, her aunt could be proud to call her niece. She looked forward to sharing her life with her family, the people she'd be tied to, proudly, for the rest of her life.

Ivy raised her glass of wine and met Ernest's eyes. He raised his glass and waited. She blinked back her tears, blinked away all her regrets.

"To family. And beginning anew," she whispered.

Ernest smiled and kissed her cheek.

Ivy knew by his expression that he realized she'd learned her lesson.

"To family," he repeated.

Staring into each other's eyes, they clinked glasses and took a sip, sealing their lives together forever with unbreakable ties.

The End

Watch for
NO WAY, Book Five and NO HOPE, Book Six
in the Spirit Creek Series coming in 2015
And
NO PEACE, a special Spirit Creek Christmas Story,
coming in November 2014

SPIRIT CREEK SERIES

historical western sweet romance,
NO MORE
NO TIME
NO CHANCE
NO TIES
NO WAY
NO HOPE

Contemporary Romance Titles

Available on Amazon.com
by Brenda Sinclair
http://www.amazon.com/-/e/B007OXHMES

LOVE TO THE RESCUE
ebook and print book available
50% of the author's royalties will be donated to Humane Society shelters

A BANDIT CREEK MIRACLE
ebook and print book available

WHEN DREAMS COLLIDE
Sequel to A Bandit Creek Miracle

Escape to Alaska Trilogy
NOT WHAT IT SEEMS
ALMOST DOESN'T COUNT
NEVER A BRIDE

COOKING FOR COWBOY
(A Stampede Sizzler)
Warning: some adult content

SECRETS FOR COWBOY
(A Stampede Sizzler,
Sequel to Cooking For Cowboy)
Warning: some adult content
ebook available through Amazon

You can find Brenda at:

Website: http://www.brendasinclairauthor.com

Facebook: http://www.facebook.com/brendasinclairauthor

Twitter: https://twitter.com/bsinclairauthor

Email: mailto:brendasinclairauthor@gmail.com

ABOUT THE AUTHOR

Brenda Sinclair is a writer of historical American West and contemporary romance, a member of her local chapter of Romance Writers of America, a healthy lifestyle advocate and past leader of her TOPS weight-loss group, a gardening enthusiast and dog lover.

Brenda was raised on a farm in southern Manitoba and taught school on a semi-remote reservation in northern Manitoba where, during frequent visits to a nearby town, she met her husband, a Treaty Cree member of the local First Nations band. She worked in the accounting field for over twenty-five years. A few years ago, she retired and traded in numbers for words when she decided to be a full-time writer.

Brenda and her husband have been married for over forty years, and during that time they raised two sons. She is extremely proud of her three wonderful grandchildren.

During writing breaks, Brenda enjoys walking the beautiful Fish Creek Park trails near her home in Calgary, Canada with her little dog, Kelly, checking out what Jack Abbott is up to on today's installment of The Young and The Restless, or snuggling with Kelly on the sofa and enjoying a good book.

Brenda believes life is good, and for days that life isn't so good, just get over it. There's always tomorrow.

34236447R00102

Made in the USA
Charleston, SC
04 October 2014